NAUGHTY WEEK

MATT DONNELLY

The following is based on a true story.
Some of the names and a few locations
have been changed at the request of the Elf B.I.

PROLOGUE

I n 1946, the Boca Raton Inn logged a reservation for a sweet older married couple from up north—somewhere very cold like Buffalo or even colder like Alaska. They were planning their vacation to Florida, something a lot of older folks from up north do during winter. They wanted to spend the week after Christmas somewhere warm, quiet, and relaxing, where no one would bother them. Most of all, they wanted to stay at a hotel for grown-ups only, a hotel that did not allow children. It's not because they didn't like children. In fact, they loved children. They had spent more than a lifetime dedicating themselves to children. But for one week out of the year, they just wanted a break. Lucky for them, it's the Boca Raton Inn's strict policy to not permit anyone under the age of twenty-one. Meaning, no kids. Ever.

On December 26, 1946, the sweet older married couple checked into the Boca Raton Inn for the very first time. Since then, every single year during the week after Christmas, the sweet older couple from up north kept a standing reservation.

Whether the staff knew exactly who was staying at their hotel between December 26 and January 1 remained a mystery. For if they did know who this sweet older married couple from up north was, then they would certainly aim to be on their absolute, very *best* behaviors.

1

CHRISTMAS 2007

Five-and-a-half year old Harrison Fulwell blinked his eyes open to find his younger brother, Max, wide awake and barely containing himself. Like many three-year-olds, Max had great difficulty waiting...for anything. Waiting was something little boys and girls are simply not qualified to do. On the day after Halloween, as soon as the Christmas decorations went up in downtown Silver Spring, Maryland, Max assumed Christmas was always a day away, every day. By comparison, Harrison, the big brother by two years, displayed exceptional patience. However, he was also old enough to know that today was finally, without a doubt, and definitively—

"Christmas!" Harrison's eyes widened and he sprang up in bed. He shuffled to the window and pushed up the vinyl shade. It was still dark outside, and frost had settled on the windowpane. For a split second it seemed to Harrison that an undisturbed blanket of snow had covered the ground on Ambler Court. He touched the cold glass of the window as the sun crested over the house across the street. As the front lawn warmed with the morning light, Harrison knew this was not to be the white Christmas he had hoped for. Immediately following that flash of disappointment was a sudden shock of anticipation. It occurred to Harrison that presents from Santa Claus, diligently wrapped by Santa's elves, were waiting underneath their Christmas tree. The only thing that stood between Harrison and Max and those presents were Mom and Dad, snoozing away in their bed.

In the master bedroom, Mom could hear floppy-socked feet thumping down the hallway. She straightened out her smile, brushed a shock of her soft brown hair over her eyes, and pretended she was asleep as the boys turned into the bedroom and jumped on the bed.

"Where's Dad?" Harrison asked. He looked toward the bathroom, but the light was off.

"Dad?!" Max exclaimed, urgently, as if he suspected Dad had already tramped downstairs ahead of them.

Mom pushed the hair from her face, opened her sleepy eyes and took in her boys—Harrison and Max, Max and Harrison. These two were everything to her. She opened up her arms and pulled Harrison and Max into her extra-snuggly embrace.

"Down here," Dad called out from the living room. There was a certain impatience to his voice. Everyone in the world knew Dad had one thing on his Christmas list. Even last night after church, he told Mr. and Mrs. Klopek, the retired neighbors across the street, how much he couldn't wait to hold his shiny new iPhone in his hands. By the sound of his voice this morning, his wish had come true.

Harrison and Max raced down the stairs as Mom trailed behind wrapping a cozy maroon bathrobe around herself. The boys stopped a distance away from the Christmas tree and took in the soft glow of the mini multi-colored lights weaving between a gentle balance of fancy and homemade ornaments. Below the tree—presents. Two small mountains of presents spilled out from

4

under the low hanging branches. Santa clearly did not have enough room under the tree. Harrison made a quick mental note —next year he would trim some additional low hanging branches.

"Merry Christmas!" Dad smiled, shooting video with his brand-new iPhone.

"Merry Christmas!" Harrison and Max belted out before scampering to the tree and tearing into the biggest packages their piles had to offer.

Dad panned the iPhone toward Mom. She was carefree and pretty, even at this early hour. She had already unwrapped a candy cane, sincerely enjoying watching her boys rip into their presents like crazy monkeys.

"Who wants candy for breakfast?!" Dad exclaimed, getting Mom's attention.

"We do!" Harrison and Max yelled, not looking away from their loot.

Mom noticed the camera was on her and playfully covered her face with her hands. Dad panned the camera back to Harrison and Max who were now holding up two Star Wars Lego sets—Harrison's 548-piece Hoth Rebel Base and Max's 244-piece AT-ST Imperial Walker.

"Awesome!" Harrison and Max's enthusiasm echoed throughout the house. Dad offered a thumbs-up, holding his thumb just within the frame of his video screen as Harrison and Max set down their new Lego sets and tore into their next largest presents.

Dad lowered his iPhone and eyed Mom with a knowing smile. She smiled back and gave a little wink as she sucked on her candy cane. It was that unspoken thing that moms and dads do that gives sons and daughters comfort even when times are tough. Harrison briefly looked up from the piles of ripped wrapping paper to notice his mom and dad smiling at each other, and a warm feeling suddenly came over him. No matter how many presents he got from Santa, no matter how big or how loud the toys, he knew in that instant he was a pretty lucky kid.

Had he known this was to be one of their last Christmases together as a family, he might have insisted on a group hug.

CHRISTMAS 2012

Harrison opened his dreary eyes and gazed across the room at an empty bed. The white glow from outside lit up the room, and Harrison could see his brother's blanket had been dragged onto the floor as if Max got out of bed in a hurry. Harrison smiled in spite of himself. He liked that his eight-year-old little brother could still get excited for Christmas. Harrison hadn't been excited for Christmas since Dad died.

He sat up in bed and looked out the window. Snow was on the ground, but it was a blue sky Christmas. The wet pavement on Ambler Court appeared black under puffy cumulus clouds. The sun shined over the neighborhood. By any standards, it was a beautiful day.

Music started playing downstairs. Harrison could barely make it out at first, but then he heard the "White Christmas" refrain. Oh no, he thought. It was the Michael Bublé Christmas album permeating through the house like the smell of peppermint and dog poop. He rolled his eyes for no one's benefit but his own. Michael Bublé meant only one thing: *Dale*.

Footsteps approached beyond the bedroom door. Harrison

pulled the covers over his head, not wanting to deal with much of anything today.

"Harrison," a woman's voice said delicately. It had been a little more than a year since they lost Dad. Mom's voice didn't sound as carefree as it once did. "Can you come downstairs now? Max can't wait much longer."

Harrison slid his legs over the side of the bed. His black sweatpants had a penny-sized hole in the knee, and his white Washington Nationals T-shirt had an orange juice stain just under the collar, but this sleep ensemble was much preferable to the brand-new generic spaceship pajamas that were trying too hard to look like Star Wars—a Christmas Eve present from Dale.

"Harrison!" his brother called from the living room.

Mom looked at Harrison expectantly as the music's volume seemed to increase.

"Dale's here?" Harrison asked.

"Let's try to have a nice Christmas." Mom turned and headed downstairs as Harrison rubbed the sleep out of his eyes and sighed. It was time to face the Michael Bublé.

THE DALE PROBLEM

Max sat impatiently by his pile of presents wearing his knock-off Star Wars pajamas. He surveyed his gifts. It wasn't a huge pile like Max remembered having when he was younger, but he was okay with it because he liked smaller toys like action figures these days. He picked up the present on top, investigated it curiously, turning it over, shaking it, weighing it against other presents. He spotted a candy cane dangling on a bent Christmas tree branch. He reached for it, but then a voice called over from the couch.

"Hmm, I don't know, buddy. Maybe not before breakfast." Dale sat cross-legged at the end of the couch, dipping a tea bag into a hot mug of water. He was wearing a green sweater and khaki corduroys with black shoes and black socks. Max thought it was weird for someone to be wearing shoes this early in the morning, especially on Christmas, but Dale was kind of a weird guy. His hair was always combed and his smile sparkled white. He didn't eat sweets because he said sugar rots teeth. He's a dentist, so he would know.

Mom scampered downstairs holding her iPhone. She wore purple yoga pants and a red tee shirt she got from her gym, but she wasn't heading out to exercise. This served as her pajamas these days. She fiddled with her phone, tapping the camera app so she could shoot video.

"Harrison, let's go, kiddo," she called before cozying up to Dale on the couch.

Harrison slugged his way down the stairs and around Mom and Dale toward the Christmas tree. He couldn't bring himself to look at Dale, who was swaying to Michael Bublé's "Holly Jolly Christmas."

"Merry Christmas, pal." Dale smiled big. If he knew how much Harrison wanted him to get swallowed up by the couch and fall into a deep pit of black tar and disappear forever, he didn't show it. Instead, he took a sip of his tea, slurping ever so slightly. To Harrison, it might as well have been the sound of a dentist's drill.

"Harrison," Mom said sternly, "don't be rude."

"Mrrh Chrsms," Harrison mumbled, still refusing to look Dale in the eye. Harrison could smell the Pillsbury cinnamon rolls baking in the oven, a Christmas tradition Mom started before Harrison was born. He wondered how many cinnamon rolls Dale was going to eat. Or if he would refuse them, citing the damaging effects sugar has on teeth. Either way, Harrison would probably hate him even more.

Two rectangular-shaped packages for Harrison and Max stood out among the others. Harrison noticed the wrapping paper, a blue background with a wide-smiling generic reindeer pattern, which differed from the piles of red and silver patterned wrapping paper—a sure sign this present came from an outside source. Max's was the same exact size, so they were likely the same exact things. Harrison didn't have to look at the little tag dangling from the silvery ribbon to know where these came from.

"Why don'tcha open mine? It's right there on top!" Even in generosity, Dale annoyed Harrison to bits. Harrison looked at the package again. He wanted to throw it in the fireplace. He wanted to heave it so hard that it would shatter against the rear bricks of the fireplace, which would allow the smaller pieces to burn more easily. From the corner of his eye, he could see Mom's extended arms, capturing everything on video. *Fine*, he thought, he'll be polite this time, but only for her. He reached for Dale's gift. Max was already tearing into his. Before Harrison could get a finger into the taped folds of the wrapping paper, Max had unveiled what might have been, historically, the worst Christmas present of all time.

"A toothbrush?" Max wondered. To say he was disappointed would have been an understatement.

"Not just any toothbrush," Dale grinned. "That there is a Sonicare 1 rechargeable electric toothbrush. It's got its own stand and everything. That's the one I use at home."

"Look at that," Mom chimed. "Dale, how thoughtful." She wrapped her arm around Dale's shoulders, appreciating the effort. "Boys, what do you say?"

"Thanks," the boys said in unison.

"You're very welcome." Dale leaned forward like he had something important to say. "And thanks to you troopers for welcoming me over for Christmas this year."

Troopers, Harrison thought. Who was Dale trying to impress? Or was he actually this lame? If Harrison cared at all, he would be embarrassed for Dale.

Harrison removed the last pieces of wrapping paper from his electric toothbrush, then lifted Max's to compare the two.

"They're exactly the same," Harrison noticed. From the couch, Dale squinted to get a better look. "What if I accidentally use Max's and Max uses mine? That's gross." Harrison had a good point. He was proud of himself for bringing it to Dale's attention.

"Don't worry about it, Harrison," Mom said. She knew Harrison had some big feelings about Dale and didn't want to make an awkward situation any more awkward.

"I can put a sticker on mine," Max piped in. Harrison shot him a look. Max's clever and quick-thinking solution to the toothbrush problem was not going to help the even greater problem that was *Dale*.

"Good idea, sport," Dale grinned. Harrison felt ganged-up on. Mom and Max were supposed to be on his side. Dale was nothing but an interloper ruining Christmas for everyone, a common enemy who seemed to have suddenly made an ally of Harrison's lifelong wingman, Max.

Something then occurred to Harrison. Something that didn't make any sense. He looked at the toothbrush again, then straight at Dale, doubling down on his opposition.

"Dad said I should never put something electric in water," Harrison stated. "Are you trying to electrocute us?" Max looked at Harrison, then at Dale. Harrison could sense the room was shifting in his favor.

"Harrison, don't be ridiculous," Mom said.

"It's completely safe, I promise," Dale assured the boys.

"Can I just keep my old toothbrush?" For Harrison, the Sonicare was more than just a gift. Had he accepted this gift, he would be accepting Dale. Harrison could not bring himself to accept Dale. Not during the second Christmas since Dad died.

"It's okay, buddy," Dale said, knowing what this was about. "Took me a little while to get used to one myself. Better safe than sorry. Let me see if I can dig up the receipt. We can take it back and pick out something else."

Harrison wondered where on earth this thing could have come from. Bed Bath & Beyond? Rite Aid? Target? Please God let it be from Target, he thought to himself. Harrison could feel

Mom staring at him. He could sense she was disappointed. He avoided eye contact, then pulled a candy cane off the tree in utter defiance.

Dale regrouped, shifting on the couch. He placed his tea on the coffee table. "Well," he said, "I have one more gift I'm hoping someone's gonna like because I can't return it." He laughed to himself, but Harrison could tell he was nervous. Dale handed Mom a long, flat box tied neatly with a bow.

"What is it, Mom?" Max wondered.

"I don't know," Mom sang in a sing-songy voice. Harrison rolled his eyes, but no one saw. He focused on smelling the cinnamon rolls, trying to keep his curiosity from getting the better of him.

Mom untied the bow, pulled off the top of the box, and peered inside. "What is this, Dale?" For a moment she seemed confused as she removed the contents from the box. "Plane tickets?" She lowered her brow curiously. Dale smiled wide, those perfectly white teeth reflecting the red, orange, and blue lights from the tree.

"Surprise!" Dale exclaimed, a nervous laugh bellowing from deep inside his lungs. Dale took a big risk with his Christmas gift to Mom, and Harrison could sense that Mom was feeling apprehensive.

"Plane tickets...for *tomorrow*?" Mom held up the rectangular, glossy white airline ticket to study it further, as if she hadn't read it clearly. Harrison couldn't believe it. Whatever Dale had done may have been miscalculated. He reached. He overshot the mark. He would certainly pay the price.

"You said you hadn't been skiing in so long," Dale added. Harrison watched closely as Dale backpedaled. Of course she hadn't been skiing, Harrison thought. There had been a very good reason for that.

Harrison shifted his eyes to Mom. She registered no clear emotion. She tilted her head slightly to one side, considering the gesture.

"Vail?" she questioned. "We're going to Vail? For a week?"

Dale smiled. His confidence was rising, and Harrison sensed it. "I figured I'd swing for the fences," Dale said. Harrison looked at Mom. Her face lightened a little, the corners of her mouth rising ever so slightly as she continued to stare at the rectangular piece of cardstock dangling between her fingertips.

Harrison could sense she was warming up to the gift. He needed to act. "I don't wanna go skiing," Harrison complained. He turned and looked Dale in the eye. "Skiing sucks." Of course he didn't really mean that. He loved skiing.

"Harrison!" Mom snapped out of her daze. "Language!"

Harrison's move backfired, and he knew it right away. He sensed Mom was anxious about traveling across the country, but his response was ineffective. If she was nervous about a plane trip, Harrison should have commented on the dangers of air travel or the tuberculosis outbreak that had been spread by passengers back in July.

"Actually, buddy," Dale said delicately, "you're not going skiing. It's just going to be your mom and me." Harrison snapped to Dale. What was he saying?

"Wait a second," Mom interrupted. "Is *this* why you were trying to reach my mother? She said you were, and I quote: 'Hounding me for my darned flourless chocolate cake recipe.' Were you planning this since November?"

Dale had a pretend look of guilt on his face. It made Harrison's stomach churn with disdain. "Well, I actually did want your mother's flourless chocolate cake recipe," Dale confessed, "but yes, I was secretly arranging this vacation for you."

"Oh Dale..." Mom was conflicted, and Harrison picked up on it. On the one hand, she had a week's long vacation with Dale.

But on the other hand, Harrison thought, it *was* a week's long vacation with Dale. In Harrison's mind, nothing could be worse than that.

Dale sat up straight, squaring his shoulders to address Harrison and Max. "You boys are going to stay with your grandma this week while your mom and I take a little trip. What do you think about that? She deserves a little vacation, right?"

Harrison and Max stared blankly at Dale as he dropped this Christmas bomb. Harrison could sense Mom's apprehension.

"Dale," she said, fanning the plane ticket. "Tomorrow?"

"I've taken care of everything," Dale reassured. "We've got a car to the airport, I've used my Amex miles so we can travel first class, and I've booked our very own chalet. Grandma will be here first thing in the morning."

For Harrison, the notion that Mom would be gone for one whole week was enough to ruin his Christmas. But now, with the reality of having to spend the entire week with Grandma slowly sinking in, it was suddenly more than Harrison could handle.

"Why do we have to stay with Grandma?" Max complained. "She makes us read her the newspaper. And she doesn't let us watch TV after seven o'clock."

"I change my mind. I want to go to Vail." Harrison pleaded desperately.

Mom sat up straight on the couch. "Boys, it's only seven days. You should be happy you get to spend a whole week with your grandmother. You don't get to see her as often now that she's traveling so much."

Harrison couldn't believe it. Did Mom just make a snap decision to abandon her children and move to Vail for one entire week with *Dale*?

"She makes us do weird chores like clean all the doorknobs in the house so she doesn't catch germs." Max was seeing this as a practical problem, which Harrison appreciated. However,

Harrison had the wherewithal to understand the larger issue here. He knew that somehow Dale was threatening his relationship with his mom, but his ten-year-old brain just didn't have the computing power to articulate his disapproval.

"She makes nasty casseroles every night," he complained.

Mom stared at her sons discontentedly. Moms have a way of projecting disappointment, sadness, love, and compassion all at once. It was a look that told Harrison and Max they had crossed a line.

"How dare you boys be so ungrateful," she said. "Grandma usually goes on her cruise this time of year, and she's giving everything up to be with you, her grandchildren. Every Christmas she gives you a card with a crisp fifty-dollar bill inside. She pours nothing but love and money into you two, and this is how you treat her?"

The guilt was being laid on as thick as cream cheese frosting. Max hanged his head. Harrison reached for another candy cane, a rebellious, however unsatisfying, attempt to regain control of the situation.

"I want you two to be on your best behavior for Grandma," Mom said. Harrison couldn't comprehend it. In an instant, the decision was made. There was no going back, and now, Harrison thought, he was expected to carry himself in a respectable manner all week long? No way. Not a chance. Not gonna happen.

"We don't have to," Harrison countered.

"Lose the attitude, mister." Mom was not going to engage in a debate. Her tone turned more stern. "You *will* be on your best behavior." Her eyes were locked on Harrison. Harrison did his absolute best to maintain eye contact, but in situations like these, deep down, he knew it was a losing battle. He dropped his eyes to the floor. But then he remembered something and squared his eye contact with Mom.

"But it's Naughty Week," Harrison said matter-of-factly.

Dale lifted his eyebrows, curious. "Naughty Week?"

Mom lowered her head and touched the tips of her fingers to her eyebrows. She closed her eyes, rubbing the skin above her nose softly.

Dale couldn't resist. "What's Naughty Week?"

4

NAUGHTY WEEK

Harrison knew he had disappointed his mother. It was one of the worst feelings in the world. But right now, in this moment, Harrison was committed. If Mom was going on vacation without him, he thought, then he must present some opposition.

Dale was still waiting for his answer about this thing called Naughty Week.

"Nothing," Mom said. "Some story their father invented."

"It's not a story. It's *real*," Harrison argued. "Every year, the week between Christmas and New Year's, kids are allowed to be bad."

"Oh yeah, why's that?" Dale's voice turned too smart-alecky for Harrison to stomach.

"Because Santa's on vacation," Harrison said with the confidence of a politician. It didn't matter whether Harrison believed his own words or not. It only mattered that Dale and Mom *thought* he believed them. "I can do whatever I want," he continued. "I can eat nothing but candy and cereal and stay up all night. I can rob a bank if I want to."

"Is that a fact?" Dale condescended.

"You will do none of those things," Mom declared, her patience thinning.

"Maybe I *will* rob a bank," Harrison said.

"Awesome!" Max couldn't help himself. The possibility of eating junk food and playing video games and maybe even robbing a bank was exciting. Harrison's wingman was back on his side.

"Rob a bank, huh?" Dale wondered. "Sounds risky. What about the cops?" Dale was only playing along, but it didn't matter to Harrison.

"I imagine the police will be busy, it being Naughty Week and all," Harrison stated.

"We'll need a getaway car," Max suggested. "And someone who knows how to drive."

"Nobody's robbing any banks!" Mom couldn't take it anymore.

Harrison tapped his finger to his nose and then pointed at Mom. "Exactly."

"So let me get this straight," Dale leaned forward, fully engaged. "During Naughty Week, Santa doesn't know if you've been good or bad because...he's on vacation?"

"Yup," Harrison nodded confidently.

"Dad said so," Max piped in.

Harrison eyed his brother. Whether the story was real, it didn't matter to Harrison. He simply used it to express some respectable ten-year-old defiance. But for Max, even though he had completely forgotten about Dad's story until this very moment, it was the Gospel truth. Because Dad said so.

Dale slurped his tea, deep in thought. "Well, yeah, then I guess it could be true," he said.

Harrison's eyebrows lifted ever so slightly. Was Dale actually agreeing with him? Mom crossed her arms and waited patiently for Dale to make his point.

"I mean, it makes sense," Dale explained. "Hard working folks need a vacation. I suppose after fifty-one weeks of very hard work up at the North Pole, Santa deserves a vacation. His elves too. I know I need a vacation every once in a while. And wouldn't you say your mom, who works so hard and raises two awesome boys, deserves a little vacation every now and then?"

Harrison was speechless. How could he argue with that? He wanted to counter with a water-tight drop-the-mic retort, but he had nothing. If he argued that his mother did *not* need a vacation, then he would seem selfish and inconsiderate. If he agreed, then the debate would be lost. If he agreed but amended the argument to suggest that she deserves a vacation but only with her children, then he knew Dale's argument would be that a vacation like that wouldn't be a vacation at all. Harrison had entered a chess match with a master chess player.

Out of coffee and out of patience, Mom finally stood. "I hate to break it to you, but there's no such thing as Naughty Week. Santa knows. Santa *always* knows when you've been good or bad. It's kind of his thing. So be good for Grandma."

Harrison looked at Dale. Then he turned to Mom. Everything else in the living room seemed to disappear—the Christmas tree, the presents, Max and the stupid electric toothbrushes. Harrison's world was about to shift dramatically. Mom was going away, thousands and thousands of miles from home, without her children.

With Dale.

Dale's gift was impressive and awfully considerate, and Harrison knew it. Somehow the goofy dentist sitting in Harrison's living room pulled it off. It hit Harrison like a giant boxing glove in the face: for the first time in Harrison's short life, Mom would be going on vacation without him.

5

MOM

I t was Christmas night, and Harrison laid in bed wide awake. Across the room, Max snoozed away. The Christmas sugar high had subsided, and Max crashed pretty hard.

But Harrison couldn't sleep. He was still bothered by the idea that his mom was going on vacation without him. He rolled over to his bedside table and reached in the little drawer. Inside were his favorite pen and markers, some souvenirs from their trip to Disneyland two years ago, and an old iPhone. It was Dad's—his Christmas present from exactly five years ago.

Harrison unlocked the screen and opened the video from Christmas morning 2007. The volume low, he watched as the younger versions of himself and Max tore through presents. He thought about how Dad helped build the Lego Hoth Rebel Base that day. Dad loved building Legos just as much as Harrison, but he never took over the project. Dad was like Harrison's assistant, making sure Harrison was on the right page of the instructions and helping find the correct pieces. Whenever Harrison got frustrated over a specific instruction, Dad steered him back on course. Harrison knew that most dads in that situation would have been tempted to just do it themselves.

"Harrison?" Mom opened the door. Harrison pulled himself up in bed as Mom sat beside him. "Did you have a nice Christmas?" She ran her fingers through Harrison's hair. Harrison thought that was such a Mom thing to do. He shrugged, indifferent about the day.

"Do you think you'll ever like Dale?" Mom asked.

"Probably not," Harrison said, eyes still glued to the iPhone.

"Do you think you could try? For me?" It was an incredibly reasonable thing to ask, and Harrison knew it. The problem for Harrison was that accepting Dale would mean, in some small way, abandoning Dad. But he also knew Dale made Mom happy.

"Can't promise anything," Harrison said, "But...maybe. For you."

Mom smiled warmly, and it radiated enough for Harrison to feel it on his cheek.

"Start it over," she said. Harrison's thumb scrubbed the video back to the beginning, and he tilted the iPhone so Mom could see better.

Mom settled next to him to watch the video. She kissed Harrison on the side of the head and hugged him close. "I miss him too."

6

GRANDMA

"Aloha, this is Geraldine, make it quick!"

It was the third time Mom called Grandma, and for the third time it went straight to voicemail. Outside, a shiny black car idled in the street, its exhaust streaming out of the tailpipe in the December cold. The sun hanged low and reflected off the windshield directly into the house.

Harrison stared out the window, silently judging the mode of transportation. The black Lincoln Town Car looked fancy, but it was no stretch limo. Harrison wondered if this was Dale's idea of luxury, or if he was just cutting costs like a cheapskate.

The driver came into view rolling two suitcases down the sidewalk. He wore a suit and tie and a thick black overcoat. It seemed like he was in a hurry, but Mom was still frantically pacing with her phone on speaker.

"Aloha, this is Geraldine, make it quick!" Harrison listened, amused. Grandma's voice had a certain youthful squakiness to it.

Harrison joined Max, perched on the stairs. "Maybe her phone died," Harrison suggested.

"Maybe she's lost," Max wondered.

"She knows where we live," Mom said, her anxiety rising through her skull.

"She could have forgotten," Harrison thought. "I mean, Grandma's old and all. Old people sometimes forget stuff, right?"

"Your grandmother will be here." Mom disappeared into the kitchen as Dale trotted downstairs with a small carry-on bag, awkwardly stepping over the boys.

"I'm sure Geraldine's just running a little late," he said. "She knows our flight's at noon. She'll be here." Harrison sensed a reduction in the confidence of his tone.

"Are you positive she knows we're leaving *today*?" Mom called from the kitchen.

Dale calmly moved into the kitchen. "She has all of the details. I confirmed with her. I guarantee she's minutes away."

Harrison and Max followed every word of the tense conversation from the stairs.

"I am not leaving this house until my mother's car is parked in the driveway." Mom was stern, yet reasonable. "I refuse to be one of those *Today Show* moms who selfishly abandons her children and then the next thing you know the house burns down."

Harrison checked the imaginary watch on his wrist. "Already past ten," he called toward the kitchen. "Prolly gonna miss your flight, huh?" Harrison knew this would only layer unnecessary tension onto an already tense situation, but he wasn't exactly going for the celebratory send-off.

Dale rubbed the frustration off his face as Harrison continued to niggle. "What a waste of first-class seats, huh Dale?"

Suddenly, Mom's phone rang. She fumbled with it, frantically trying to answer. "It's Mom. Finally." She placed it on speakerphone as she hurried to the window. "Mom...Mom? You're breaking up, I can't hear you."

The phone chirped unintelligibly. "Where are you?" Mom pushed on, "I said, WHERE ARE YOU?" Mom's annoyance turned to frustration. Next, logically, she'd turn angry, and Harrison didn't want to be around for that. He considered heading upstairs.

Dale opened the front door and gave the driver of his affordable Lincoln Town Car a "five minutes" wave.

And that's when Harrison heard it—the low rumble of the rusted muffler under a 1985 white Toyota Tercel. It was Grandma's car, and it grew louder as it approached.

When it pulled onto Ambler Court, Max jumped up. "Grandma!"

Grandma honked twice as she pulled into the driveway. "Ha!" Dale yawped. "She's here!"

Grandma's car shut off. Dale watched from the front door. Every second that passed was like a screw tightening in his brain. Finally the driver's side door flung open and out hopped Grandma.

"Never fear, Grandma is here!" Grandma bellowed into the neighborhood. She was in her sixties, but her hair was impossibly blonde. She stood a head taller than Harrison, and her skin was orange. She wore large, dark sunglasses and had her cell phone mounted on her hip, which poked out under a heavy gray hooded sweatshirt. In her ear was a state-of-the-art Bluetooth device. She waved two envelopes at the house. "Where are my favorite little buggers?!"

Dale turned inside the house and squared up with Mom. "Can we go now?" he said, deeply relieved.

"I know I'm forgetting something." Mom checked the list on her phone again. She was an avid list-maker.

"Don't worry, we have everything," Dale insisted.

"Sorry about the phone call," Grandma said as she climbed the three short stairs to the front door. "I'm testing out the new Bluetooth."

"My passport!" Mom headed for the stairs.

"We're going to Colorado," Dale reasoned.

"I always travel with my passport. I'll be two minutes," she said as she disappeared in the upstairs hallway.

Dale sighed heavily. "I'll meet you in the car!"

"Merry Christmas, daughter!" Grandma yelled upstairs. She pulled the Bluetooth device out of her ear and showed it to Dale. "I wanted the LG, but Stanley swears by Plantronics." She cut herself off suddenly and looked up at Dale. "Daley-boy, I didn't forget. I've got that flourless chocolate cake recipe I promised you. Mind if I e-mail a PDF?" Grandma took a certain pride in her tech savviness.

"That's fine, Geraldine." Harrison could tell Dale didn't like being called "Daley-boy."

"Best you ever had," she stated. "Won Best Alternative Cake at the Leisure World Autumn Bake-Off back in 2010." She found Harrison and Max on the stairs and smiled wide. Her teeth gleamed in contrast with her face's tangerine hue.

"Thank you, Geraldine, for everything," Dale said sincerely. "And have a great week."

"Oh I plan on it," she stated as she approached her grandsons.

"Hold down the fort, fellas," Dale said, hustling out the door. It was an awkward goodbye, but Dale couldn't wait any longer.

"Be right there!" Mom called from upstairs, frantically searching for her passport.

Grandma opened her arms, and Harrison and Max leaned toward her. She pulled the boys in tight and smothered them with kisses. She pulled back and presented the envelopes.

"One for you," she handed an envelope to Max, "and one for you." Harrison accepted his gift, knowing exactly what was inside. "Merry Christmas, my dears," she said through her shiny white smile. "Buy something loud and obnoxious. Now if you'll excuse me, I need to use the ladies room. Stanley's got me on a liquid breakfast. Between that and the coffee, boy I tell ya."

Grandma wandered toward the bathroom. Harrison and Max tore into their cards, unveiling two crisp fifty-dollar bills.

"Don't forget your thank-you notes." Mom rushed down the stairs, passport in hand. At the bottom of the stairs, she turned and hurriedly kissed Harrison and Max goodbye. "It's only a week. Be good for Grandma," she said. "Don't do anything illegal or stupid and ruin my vacation." She was joking but maybe only half-joking. She looked at Harrison squarely in the eye. "I love you," and then to Max, "I love you." She stood tall and turned toward the bathroom. "Bye, Mother! Thank you!" she shouted.

In the bathroom, Grandma was standing in front of the mirror, one finger steadying her Bluetooth device and the other finger pressed to her other ear. "Stanley? Stan, baby, I'm in the powder room...I don't know, maybe it's the battery." Between the digital distortion in her ear, the door being closed, the automatic light-and-fan combination running overhead, and the thirty-three Barry Manilow concerts Grandma had attended in her sixty-plus years of life, there was *zero* chance that she heard her daughter say goodbye.

Mom opened the front door, then turned back to her boys. The Lincoln Town Car honked sheepishly, but Mom ignored it. She stepped toward her boys and wrapped them into a hug.

"Best behaviors," she said, pulling away and dabbing the moisture out of her right eye. "Got it?"

Harrison and Max nodded, and Mom was out door. The boys moved to the frosted window and watched as Mom got in the Town Car and the car motored away.

"I guess we should start cleaning the doorknobs," Max suggested, a certain surrender in his voice.

"This week is gonna stink." Harrison was beyond surrender. He was downright depressed.

Grandma burst from the bathroom, finger still to her Bluetooth device. "Ruthie, relax, I just got off the horn with him. Had to make a pit stop to see the fam, but I'm on my way!" She clicked off her Bluetooth and yelled upstairs: "Dear daughter, I wish I could stay for lunch, but as you know I have a plane to catch! Carnival Cruises waits for no one! See you in a week!"

Max looked at Harrison, confused. Harrison was himself utterly confused.

"Have a fun week, my dears," Grandma said, going for the unpolished doorknob of the front door. "Don't be afraid to get into a little trouble," she winked. She started out the door, then popped her head back inside the house. "See you boys in the new year!"

And she left, closing the door behind her.

Inside the house, the silence settled in. The only sound was the airflow blowing warm from the floor-level vents. Harrison looked out the window as Grandma piled into her car and started the engine.

"Grandma!" Max shouted instinctively. He wasn't accustomed to being so suddenly unsupervised. Just as instinctively, Harrison elbowed Max in the arm.

"Ow! What was that for?"

Harrison leaned forward until his forehead tapped the chilly window pane of the window, watching as Grandma's car rattled away. He turned and stared at Max, processing what had just happened, the gears in his ten-year-old brain spinning wildly.

"She's coming back, right?" Max wondered.

Harrison couldn't believe his great fortune, but it seemed that it was actually happening. As improbable as it might have been, it was absolutely definitely happening. His pensive face smiled wide.

"No," he stated with authority. "We're on our own."

DECEMBER 26, 2012

Harrison sat on the edge of his bed and slid on his gray Gore-Tex ski pants. He was already wearing his long sleeve long john undershirt and navy-blue Henley. He pulled on his snow boots and zipped the pant cuffs around them, then stood tall to view himself in the mirror.

He looked pretty darned sharp, he thought.

The ensemble was purchased last year. Harrison remembered the pants being too big on him when he, his mom, and Max drove up to Seven Springs for a weekend ski trip. Dad had always wanted the boys to ski. He absolutely loved skiing. He viewed it as one of those activities that required a human being to be so harmoniously in tune with nature, like surfing or rock climbing. And he would always state that he was pretty good, but Mom was even better because she was so naturally athletic.

Dad met Mom on a ski trip. Harrison and Max had heard the story a gazillion times. It was during Mom and Dad's senior year of college. They had both gone to the University of Maryland but somehow their paths never crossed. Then during the autumn of 1999, they each came across a flyer printed on blue paper and stapled to a large, circular kiosk. There was a special deal for a trip to Seven Springs Mountain Ski Resort. If someone could convince five or more friends to commit to lodging and lift tickets, that person's trip would be free. Within days of one another, Mom and Dad had each torn off a little strip of paper with a phone number and started working on their friends. The next thing they knew, fate had delivered them to side-by-side ski chalets on the same Pennsylvania mountain for the New Year's weekend over winter break, and their lives were changed forever.

As Harrison stared at himself in the mirror, he wondered that maybe, deep down, the reason he had been so stubbornly defiant with his mom and Dale was because he just didn't like the idea that Mom and Dale were going on a ski trip. Skiing was Mom and Dad's thing. After hearing their story so many times, it held a sacred place in Harrison's heart.

Harrison blinked, trying to put it out of his mind. He moved for his closet and pulled out a large, puffy red ski jacket. He slid it on and zipped it up. He found a blue ski hat and ski goggles but then tossed them aside for the scuffed white football helmet on the floor of the closet. He gripped the facemask with his fingers and headed downstairs.

When Harrison exited the house, he deliberately left the front door open. Was he trying to heat the entire neighborhood? Maybe. Harrison didn't care. It was Naughty Week after all.

Outside, a ladder leaned against the house, standing in the gap between two soft bushes covered in snow. Harrison placed the helmet on his head as he tramped across the snow. At the base of the ladder, he looked up toward the sky.

He gauged the distance from the roof to the ground. It was pretty high. He knew a basketball hoop was ten feet high, so if he were to guess, the lip of the roof was about twenty feet up. He had a slight fear of heights, but he knew if he was going to make the most of Naughty Week, then he'd need to step out of his comfort zone.

He started up the aluminum rungs of the ladder, gripping each rung with his padded ski gloves and pulling himself toward the top. If any grown-up neighbors were watching, they would probably think he was taking down Christmas decorations.

At the top of the ladder, Harrison hefted himself up and over the gutter and crawled forward until he could get to his feet. Powdery snow rolled off the roof and dropped to the soft bushes below. Balancing himself on the angled roof, Harrison looked around. The neighborhood was beautiful from this vantage point. Bare trees coated in ice, untouched white snow blanketing rooftops, the Crayola blue sky in contrast overhead.

He carefully side-stepped his way up the roof, placing his feet parallel with the angular slope and shimmying up as not to slip and fall. It was a skier's trick he learned during his first ski trip with Mom and Dad. He remembered skiing a bunny slope, coming down the hill slowly, skis angled to a point to control his speed. He had accidentally dropped a ski pole and needed to stop and climb up the mountain a little ways to retrieve it. Instead of fully removing his skis, which could be a time-consuming and cumbersome maneuver, Dad taught him to turn his skis so they were parallel with the slope and side step up the mountain.

Harrison arrived at the very top of the roof and started packing snowballs just as Max wandered out of the house. He wore an oversized sweatshirt under a kitchen apron. He had yellow rubber gloves covering his hands and held a green canister of disinfectant wipes. He saw the ladder and looked toward the roof, shielding his eyes from the brightness of the sky.

"Harrison?" he called up, wandering toward the sidewalk to get a better view. The closer to the street Max headed, the more of the roof he could see.

Harrison spotted Max as he came into view. "Look out below!"

Harrison announced.

THWAP! A snowball landed a Max's feet.

"What the heck are you doing?" Max yelled up at his brother.

"What the heck does it look like I'm doing? I'm protecting our castle!"

"From what?!" Max yelled.

"Cars!" Harrison yelled back. At the end of Ambler Court, a mail truck drove past. Harrison threw a snowball as far as he could, but it fell short of the street.

"You can't do that!" Max called up at Harrison.

"Oh yeah? Who's gonna stop me? You? Mom? All the way from Vail?"

"She left a message from the airport," Max stated, as if that would be enough to stop Harrison from causing mayhem from the roof and return to level ground.

"So what?" Harrison yelled. "For all she knows, we're at the movies with Grandma." Harrison's train of thought went off course for a moment. He thought about the last time Grandma took them to the movie theater. For all her quirks, she had pretty awesome taste. She took them to see a movie called *Super 8*. It gave Harrison nightmares for a week, but it was so worth it.

"But Grandma left for her cruise." Max still didn't fully comprehend the reality of their situation.

"Duh," Harrison said. "And now we're all alone. And we're gonna keep it that way because *this* is the very definition of Christmas vacation. No school, no chores, and no parental super-vision! It's the greatest gift of all! So look out."

"You're gonna slip and fall and break your leg!" Max warned.

THWAP! Another snowball landed near Max's feet. Harrison laughed heartily and suddenly lost balance, nearly falling on his butt. He caught himself, carefully lowered himself to his knees, and continued packing snowballs.

"I'm calling Mom," Max threatened. The thought of being

alone all week was pretty cool, but what's the point of having no parental supervision if his brother was in the hospital with a broken leg?

"Go ahead. Call Mom," Harrison yelled. "But do you know what will happen next?" Harrison pointed across the street. "As soon as she finds out that Grandma confused the dates and left us all alone, Mom will make us go to Mrs. Klopek's house. Do you wanna go to Mrs. Klopek's house? Do you wanna smell like chicken soup for the rest of the week?"

Max turned and looked at the single-level home on the other side of their street. He thought about those times they had to spend the afternoon with Mrs. Klopek when Dad was in the hospital. There was nothing to do except make puzzles. Mrs. Klopek had about twenty puzzles, and they were all puppy themed. Staying with Mrs. Klopek would have been a hundred times worse than spending the week with Grandma. Harrison knew that, and Harrison knew that Max knew that.

"Fine," Max surrendered. "But if you slip off the roof and break your arms and legs, then no one's gonna care because you are sooooo gonna be in trouble." It was a last-ditch effort to entice Harrison down from the roof.

"You're wrong, Maxy. It's Naughty Week. We're allowed to be bad."

"Mom said there's no such thing as Naughty Week."

"That's just what she wants us to believe," Harrison said. "Can you imagine if we were given total freedom to do whatever we wanted? Mom wouldn't stand a chance. Anyway, Dad never lied to us."

Harrison made a strong point. The question for Max now was which parent should he trust? On the one hand, Mom wouldn't want them to have the freedom to do whatever they wanted for one whole week. It goes against every single one of a parent's protector instincts. But on the other hand, why would Dad tell them about Naughty Week if it weren't true? Then Max remembered their dad had in fact lied to them before.

"He lied to us about getting better," Max pointed out, sadly.

"Shut up, butt face!" Harrison had had enough. He tossed a snowball and—THWAP—knocked the disinfectant wipes out of Max's hand as a thick, marshmallowy cloud drifted in front of the sun, making visibility on the roof flat and even.

And that's when something caught Harrison's attention.

On the chimney, stuck between two bricks, a white sheet of paper fluttered in the breeze. By the looks of it, it had not been there very long. Harrison squinted at it. It was already odd to be on the roof with no parental supervision, but for some reason finding a random piece of paper stuck in the chimney was particularly strange.

Harrison shimmied over to the chimney and reached for the paper. Freeing it from the crack, he smoothed it out and looked it over, unsure of what he had discovered. At the top of the page was a banner ad for Alaskan Airlines, and below that was a name, e-mail address, date, and subject line.

"What are you looking at?" Max shouted impatiently.

Harrison's eyes continued down the page. "It's a travel confirmation," he stated.

"Aw man, is it Dale's? He's gonna be so ticked."

Harrison took a closer look. Some of the information didn't make sense. He would have taken a little enjoyment if Dale had lost his travel itinerary. He's usually so together and organized. But the destination on this itinerary was Florida, not Colorado, so it couldn't be Dale's.

Harrison squinted at the e-mail address. He looked at the details of the flight. He studied the name of the travelers.

And then his eyes widened, like he just found a long-lost treasure map.

"HAHA I KNEW IT!" Harrison exclaimed, victoriously lifting

the paper into the sky. The momentum of his arm swinging into the air forced his footing to shift ever so slightly, causing a chain reaction throughout his body. His feet slipped, and he backflopped onto the snowy roof. He slid down toward the edge, flailing his arms and desperately trying to grab hold of something as he fell. His speed picked up, and Harrison twisted as he went over the edge. His fingers took hold of the gutter, and his legs swung down, boots clapping the side of the house.

He had caught himself. Somehow, some way, he was not falling the twenty feet to certain death. He looked up at his grip. The paper was trapped between his right hand and the frozen gutter. His left hand shifted wider, evening the balance of weight. Snow trickled into the the cuff of his sleeve and nearly made it all the way down to his elbow. And then three pre-packed snowballs rolled over the edge and popped Harrison in the face.

Harrison shook the powdery snow off his red cheeks and forehead and looked over to his right. There, taunting him, was the ladder, seemingly a mile away. Harrison thought about swimming lessons. Back when he was learning to swim, the lifeguard's advice if Harrison ever got in trouble was to put his head down and kick toward the edge. Once he made it to the edge, he should find the pool ladder and "monkey crawl" over to safety. Harrison tried monkey crawling his way toward the ladder, but his body was significantly heavier than it would be in a pool, and the football helmet and winter clothes added extra weight. He wasn't sure if he could make it to the ladder. He especially didn't want to let go of the travel confirmation he just found. And then, as his right arm reached over, he suddenly lost his grip and—

"Aaaaaagh!" Harrison dropped into a soft, snowy bush.

"Harrison!" Max hurried over, "Are you okay? Are you dead?"

From the depths of the powdery bush, an unbroken arm shot out victorious, grasping the sheet of paper like an Olympic gold medal.

8

TRAVEL CONFIRMATION E6437

Harrison warmed himself on the living room couch. His red puffy coat and football helmet were on the floor. In the few short hours since Mom and Dale left, the place had already been overrun by feral boys. Half-eaten bowls of cereal loitered on the coffee table, spilled bags of chips on the floor, and holiday-colored candy wrappers were strewn everywhere else. The television played with the volume turned down low. It was tuned to one of those midday judge shows, but it didn't matter because no adult was around to tell the boys to turn it off.

Max drank straight out of a two-liter bottle of Sprite as Harrison stood up and started pacing. He held the travel confirmation in his hands like a treasure map.

"I knew it," he kept saying. "I knew it I knew it I knew it!" He had a big smile on his face. "I mean, I didn't *know* it...but I knew it!"

Max belched. It was long and loud and good. "What did you know?" he asked, taking another gulp of room temperature Sprite.

"Naughty Week," Harrison said pointedly, holding up the itinerary. "This proves everything. I mean....*everything*."

The gears in Harrison's brain churned uncontrollably, for this otherwise insignificant e-mail printout of a travel itinerary meant so much more than some stranger's travel plans. All evidence pointed to one thing: Harrison held the travel plans of Nicholas Claus, a.k.a. Santa Claus, which meant Jolly Old Saint Nicholas was on vacation.

"It could be a fake," Max suggested. With only a few hours of total independence under his belt, Max had turned surprisingly sensical.

Harrison did have some skepticism too. He wondered if the thing that made him so sure he was holding the flight information for Santa Claus's post-Christmas vacation was that he wanted it so much to be true. The mind has a powerful way of steering one's desires. But then something occurred to him.

"Nobody fakes a travel itinerary," he stated. Even as the words uttered from his mouth, it sounded ridiculous. Who would do that?

"I bet Dale's playing a trick on us," Max said. Very often, Harrison and Max's relationship had a yin and yang sort of balance. If one was misbehaving for Mom, then the other acted like an angel. If one didn't like the new chicken recipe Mom tried for dinner, the other was all compliments. It struck an odd balance between the siblings, but it was a balance nonetheless.

"Dale's waaaaay too boring to pull off something this epic." Harrison made a good point. First of all, it would have been very clever of Dale to fake Santa's itinerary, but perhaps not out of the question. But Dale would not have been crafty enough to lodge it way up there on the chimney. He'd have had to anticipate that Harrison or Max would climb up to the roof, and even Dale was smart enough to know that Mom wouldn't approve of that.

"Check this out," Harrison shook the paper at Max. "The e-mail address...NickClaus1823@yahoo.com." He quietly chuckled to himself. "How about that, Santa's a Yahoo man."

"Anybody can make up a phony e-mail address," Max argued.

Harrison was starting to lose patience. He appreciated Max's skepticism to a point. "Max, I'm sick of your negativeness. You must've gotten it from Mom because it certainly didn't come from Dad."

For Harrison, the travel itinerary meant three things. First of all, it confirmed that Santa Claus was the real deal. Harrison had started to have doubts back in December of third grade. He wondered things like, *How does one person deliver presents to all the children of the world in one night?* And *How can the elves possibly make a Sony PlayStation in Santa's workshop?* It didn't quite add up.

That year, on Christmas Eve, Harrison finally went to the authority on the matter. He knew Dad would give it to him straight, even though he hadn't been feeling well for a little while. Harrison mustered his strength and approached Dad, who was lying on the couch under a blanket watching *It's A Wonderful Life* on TV. Bottles of medicine stood on the coffee table next to a tall glass of water. Dad had started feeling a little better since he began taking the pills. He had to take a lot of pills though.

"Dad," Harrison asked gently but assertively. "There's no such thing as Santa, right?"

Dad raised his thin brown eyebrows and sat up. He patted the spot next to him so Harrison could sit.

"What do you think?" Dad asked.

Harrison stared at the TV. He had been debating this in his head for the last two weeks, and he finally wanted some clarity. But he also strangely liked not knowing. Did it even matter? If Santa wasn't real, would Christmas be any different? On the other hand, what if Santa *did* exist? He would certainly know that Harrison was doubting. Would Harrison be penalized for this come Christmas morning? Harrison was deeply conflicted.

"I don't think he's real," Harrison finally stated, eyes lowered. He felt ashamed and embarrassed, even though he knew there was nothing to feel ashamed and embarrassed about. Then he got a little sad, like he was mourning the loss of a friend.

"Aw, that's too bad," Dad said, sniffling through some congestion. "Because I know for a fact Santa is real."

Harrison looked up at his dad. *What did he just say?* There was something in the casualness of Dad's tone that instantly made Harrison second-guess his festering doubt. Now he was just confused.

"You've seen him?" Harrison asked, wanting so badly for it to be true.

"Well, no, I haven't ever seen him. But I've heard him a few times. Just last year, there was this thud on the roof and it woke me up. Then I heard footsteps, and suddenly there was some rustling in the living room. I was pretty disoriented, having just woken up, but as soon as I caught my bearings, everything turned quiet as a mouse."

Dad stared ahead at the TV, watching as young George Bailey passed out sodas to kids in the pharmacy. Harrison processed the new information. Why hadn't Dad mentioned this before?

"Besides," Dad continued, "I can't explain how presents from Santa to you boys get under the tree every year. That must count for something, right?"

"You still believe in Santa?" Harrison asked his father, point-blank.

"Absolutely," Dad said. "There's no doubt in my mind."

Harrison's faith was restored that Christmas, but that was to be the last Christmas Harrison believed in Santa Claus. That was also the last Christmas with Dad. The following year, it didn't matter whether Santa existed. Nothing mattered that Christmas. Dad was gone. It was a very sad time.

Harrison studied the travel itinerary as he considered what

else it meant. Not only had it proven Santa was real, but it also confirmed something else Dad was so certain about. It had confirmed that Santa Claus and Mrs. Claus did in fact take a vacation right after Christmas. And why wouldn't they? It made perfect sense. After fifty-one weeks of grinding it out for the children of the world, the big guy deserved a little rest. And that meant if Santa was on vacation the week between Christmas and New Year's, then Naughty Week was *real*.

Harrison's eyes widened. Even though the travel itinerary had undeniably confirmed Santa's existence, and it had suggested beyond a reasonable doubt that Naughty Week was real, there was one more thing this piece of paper meant, perhaps the most important thing of all.

It meant that Dad had *not* lied.

Harrison's heart warmed.

"I don't know," Max said. Harrison could tell his brother was still skeptical. And why shouldn't he be? In the fourteen months since the boys lost their father, their lives had changed so dramatically. In an instant they witnessed the sudden and devastating shattering of their mother's spirit. After Dad died, everything they did would be a first—the first time skiing without Dad, the first time eating McDonald's without Dad, the first Fourth of July without Dad. The first Christmas.

And then Mom met Dale, and things got even more confusing. He was a nice guy, friendly and respectful. For Max, everything felt new and different. Change is hard, especially for an eight-year-old, and Harrison knew that.

"Look," Harrison started, "do you believe in Santa Claus?"

"Yes," Max affirmed. There was no doubt in his mind, itinerary or no itinerary.

"Do you believe Santa brings you presents on Christmas Eve?" Harrison continued.

"Yes," Max stated the obvious.

"Do you believe he spends the entire year making presents for all eighty billion kids on the planet?"

"Well, yeah, but he has help." Max reasoned. "And it's not all eighty billion kids. He only delivers presents to the kids who believe."

Harrison appreciated Max's rationale. "Sure he does," Harrison said. "He has help from the elves." The words surprised him as they came out of his mouth, his faith so expeditiously restored. "But then think about it," he continued. "Doesn't it make sense for Santa and those hardworking elves to take a vacation just one week out of the year? And wouldn't it be logical for them to go on vacation right after the most important day on the North Pole calendar?"

Max considered this momentarily. He folded one arm across his chest, resting his other elbow on top, and tapped his lips with his pointer finger.

And then he smiled, and his eyes shined under his overgrown mop of hair.

"Dad was right. Naughty week *is* real."

9

THE SANTA CLAWS CAT BURGLAR

The excitement that Naughty Week was a reality had settled in, and Harrison and Max were enjoying day one. Every television in the house was on because the boys could think of no reason to turn them off. In the kitchen, the small TV mounted on the wall was tuned to the local evening news.

Seven freshly delivered pizzas stood neatly stacked in white boxes on the stovetop—one for every day of Naughty Week. Harrison figured since he was in charge and could do whatever he wanted, he could order food for the whole week now to save money on one tip instead of tipping the driver every day they got food delivered. He sat on the edge of the kitchen counter, feeling proud of himself for his sensible choice and eating a large slice of cheese pizza. Beside him stood a two-liter bottle of Sprite with his name on it written in black permanent marker.

Max helped himself to some pizza. He slid two piping hot slices on his plate and tore a paper towel off the roll. Then he grabbed the two-liter bottle of Sprite that had his name on it.

"I can't believe you're using a plate," Harrison said. "What a tool."

"I can't believe you think seven pizzas is gonna last us 'til next week," Max replied. "We only have like twenty dollars left, and we're almost out of soda."

Max had always been a worrier. His anxiety rose over the most insignificant things. Harrison remembered the time that Max totally melted down when there was only enough Honey Bunches of Oats for a half a bowl of cereal. The tantrum that followed was so loud and so strong that Mrs. Klopek walked across the street to see what was the matter. Maybe this would be the week that Max learned to relax and enjoy the freedoms of life, Harrison thought.

The boys' attention was turned to the television where a curious police sketch filled the screen. It was a long-faced, pencil-smudged rendering of a bearded man wearing a Santa hat.

"Hey, looks like Santa's in trouble," Max said.

"That's not Santa," Harrison said with a mouthful of pizza.

On the lower third of the screen, text appeared—*Breaking News: Santa Claws cat burglar strikes again.*

Harrison reached for the remote and turned up the volume.

"...curiously emancipating the cuddly critters from area animal shelters, exchanging them for valuables in each burglarized home, leaving a trail of tears...and of cats," the news anchor lady stated.

The news transitioned to an interview where a tearful six-year-old girl clung to a mangy tabby-like mixed breed. "He took our TV but he left this cat and I love her and her name is Bobo but my daddy says I can't keep her," the child blubbered.

The news anchor lady appeared on screen to wrap up the story. "This afternoon we've received reports of a break-in at an animal shelter in Rockville. Montgomery County residents are advised to be especially cautious over the next few days and to contact local authorities if—"

Harrison muted the TV and dropped the remote on the counter.

"Oh!" Max exclaimed, "I get it. 'Santa Claws.' He's a cat burglar, right? And he leaves cats at the houses he burglars." Max chuckled to himself.

"*Burglarizes,*" Harrison corrected. "Yeah, I get it. It's not that funny."

"Well, according to you, he's not doing anything wrong because it's Naughty Week."

Harrison stared at Max. His little brother once again surprised him with some very streamlined logical thinking. But there was a tiny flaw to Max's logic. "You're a hundred percent right," Harrison said. "But the thing is, he started cat burglaring like two weeks ago. So he's totally on the Naughty List."

"*Burglarizing,*" Max corrected, proud of himself.

"Shut up." It was all Harrison could think to say. A boy can grow and mature, but a big brother can never outgrow his big brother-ness.

Max chugged down the rest of his Sprite and tossed the empty plastic bottle toward the recycle bin, missing badly. The bottle bounced across the floor of the kitchen.

"So what happens when we run out of money?" Max asked.

"Don't worry about money," Harrison said.

"Why not?"

"Because I'm gonna rob a bank." Harrison's confidence surprised Max.

"No way," Max said. Harrison had to have been messing with him.

"Yes way. I already started drawing up plans."

Harrison opened the greasy lid of a pizza box where a crudely drawn blueprint was sketched on the inside in black permanent marker. Max looked closely. There was a long rectangular section labeled "Teller." Behind that was a square area labeled "Vault."

"You can't rob a bank! That's stealing!"

"Chill out, dip-wad," Harrison said. "I'm not gonna steal anything." He was, in fact, just messing with Max. "Mom left an envelope of cash for Grandma. There's like two hundred dollars in there."

Max's anxiety subsided. Two hundred dollars was plenty to get through the week. He was a pretty good math student, and from his early estimates, he would have all the soda he could drink.

"Still," Harrison mused, "it would be pretty cool to rob a bank, even if we didn't steal anything. Like that time we went fishing with Dad and threw back the fish."

"I don't know," Max said. "I don't think the cops care if it's Naughty Week. Just ask the Santa Claws Cat Burglar. I mean, he'll be captured eventually, right?"

Suddenly a loud CRASH shook the house. Harrison and Max looked at one another.

What was that?!

10

THE VISITOR

"What the heck is that?" Max's voice shook as he stared at the ceiling.

"Something on the roof," Harrison stated the obvious.

Max's face whitened. "Do you think it's the Santa Claws Cat Burglar?"

Harrison looked at his little brother dismissively. It was so much like a third grader to jump to conclusions based on recent information. Harrison wondered if he should go around the house and turn off all of the TVs. With no adult supervision and Max's high anxiety, it could be a long week.

"Harrison!" Max shouted, trying to snap his big brother out of it.

"Shhhh!" Harrison quietly started out of the kitchen.

"Where are you going?" Max whispered.

Harrison turned back. He pointed two fingers at his eyes, then two fingers at Max, then up toward the roof—his interpretation of military-style sign language. It made no sense to Max, but he nodded anyway. Harrison grabbed the broom from the little nook by the kitchen doorway and headed out. Max followed, grabbing the dustpan.

"What are you gonna do with that?" Harrison whispered.

Max shrugged. Then suddenly there was a rattling and clattering. It was loud and irritating, like some raccoons were outside getting into the trash cans and there was absolutely nothing anyone could do about it because of rabies, of course.

"Naughty Week or not," Max worried, "I'm calling the police."

"Yeah, maybe we should."

They hustled into the living room, heading straight for the phone. Before they could dial 911, there was more rattling, and a high-pitched *YEEEEE-AAAAAAAAH!*

And then a THUD.

A cloud of dust and ash billowed from the fireplace, followed by...nothing. Silence.

Harrison moved across the living room to investigate.

"Harrison," Max whispered, holding the phone receiver.

"Shh." Harrison's shushing was sharp and urgent.

Max followed closely behind, wielding the dust pan like a weapon as the debris from the fireplace settled.

"What is it?" Max asked, unable to get a clean line of sight.

"It's..." Harrison trailed off, not a hundred percent sure what he was seeing. He could barely string a sentence together. "It's... it's...it's an elf."

Max moved beside Harrison to get a better view. They both leaned forward. There, before them, in the flesh, lay a small, elfish woman with elfish features wearing elf-sized but otherwise normal clothing: khaki corduroy pants with a dark green cashmere sweater wrapped in a black pea coat. She wore polished black leather boots with thick soles that offered some extra height. If she wasn't so elfish, she'd look like a teacher. Her hair was long and blonde under a cream-colored beanie. Her cheeks had turned rosy from the cold, and her forehead was smudged with soot from the fireplace.

She appeared nonthreatening at the moment, but that was likely due to her being out cold, snoozing like a puppy after a long walk. Harrison and Max relaxed.

"She's totally knocked out," Harrison bemused.

"Why is she in our living room?" Max wondered. It was a terrific question.

Harrison caught Max's gaze with a mischievous smile. "I guess there's only one way to find out."

11

GEORGE

Max dragged a chair from the dining room into the kitchen as Harrison hustled in from the garage with three bungee cords. Harrison disappeared into the living room and returned a moment later carrying their sleeping elfish guest in his arms. She weighed about the same as an adult Boston Terrier with a weight problem, about thirty pounds. He gently placed her in the chair. Still unconscious, her head nodded to one side. Max snapped a few times in front of her face, and she murmured some indecipherable words mixed with grunts.

"She's waking up," Max said as Harrison knotted the bungee cords around her torso and legs.

Max was a little confused by what Harrison was doing. "Do you really think that's necessary?"

Harrison finished tying the bungee cords and stepped back. "Of course it's necessary," he said. "She's an intruder."

The elf-woman's eyes fluttered open. Disoriented and confused, she blinked a few times to regain her senses. She looked back and forth from Harrison to Max.

And then she SCREAMED. Harrison and Max screamed too. After a long breath of screaming, all three stopped at the same time.

"Who are you?" Harrison interrogated.

"I'm George, who the heck are you?" she said.

Harrison and Max looked at one another. Did she just say *George*?

"Your name is George?" Harrison asked.

"You got jellycake in your ears? Yes, George, my name is George. All my life. It was the name given to me upon my birth. People get names down here, don't they?" She was brash and impatient, and the sound of her voice suggested maybe she was from Chicago. But perhaps her irritation stemmed from her being in a strange place bound to a chair. She looked at the bungee cords, then looked at the boys. She zeroed in on Max who appeared to be the less threatening of the two. His overgrown hair had fallen over one eye like a flap. "Say, flappy, do me a solid and untie me, would ya?"

Max pushed the hair out of his eyes and looked at Harrison who had his arms folded across his chest.

"I don't think so," Harrison said.

"And why the heck not?" For an elf, George was rather abrasive.

"I think *we'll* be asking the questions," Harrison stated, leaning forward for emphasis.

"Are you sure about that?" George questioned.

It occurred to Harrison what George was doing. "Stop it," he demanded.

"You want me to stop?" she asked. "You want me to stop asking questions?" It had not only turned into an obnoxious game, it was a power struggle.

"What are you doing here?" Harrison asked.

"Well," George started, "what do you think I'm doing here?" The power struggle continued.

"You're a cat burglar trying to rob us!" Max exclaimed. His senses were on high alert ever since he watched the news report on the Santa Claws Cat Burglar.

"Now that's just silly," George dismissed. "I'm hardly big enough to be a cat."

"So what are you?" Harrison pressed.

"What's it look like, pal?"

Harrison squinted at her. She had an annoying talent for being able to ask questions under any circumstance.

"You're an elf," he said with the ninety percent confidence of a police detective.

"Hand that man a mini chop!" George celebrated sarcastically. "He just answered correctly! Now will someone untie me before I pee my pants?" George squirmed in her bindings, barely able to move. "Wow, you guys did good. I mean, pretty decent handiwork. What is this? Sheepshank? Bowline?" Those were the only kinds of knots George knew.

"Are you gonna tell us why you're here? Or should we just call the police?" Harrison upped the ante, which grabbed George's attention.

"Whoa, whoa, whoa," George pleaded, "I am on a mission of peace. No need to involve the authorities here." George looked around the kitchen, then turned to Max. "Say, where's your folks, flappy?"

"My mom is in Vail skiing," Max started, "and my dad—"

Harrison elbowed Max. It was none of her business what had happened to their father. She could only use that information to her advantage. Max rubbed the soreness out of his upper arm as George nodded. She had all the information she needed.

"Okay," George stated, "so I *am* at the right house. I was a little worried for a minute there." She suddenly lost all train of thought as her senses fully restored. "HEEEEEEY do I smell pizza?"

The seven pizza boxes were still stacked on the stove top behind George. She craned her neck and tried to pivot her body to get a better look. "Aw man," she said, "is that pepperoni?"

"Yeah," Max confirmed. "Want some?"

George turned to Max appreciatively. "Thanks, flappy. We don't get a lot of good pizza up at the North Pole. And lower forty-eight pie is bomb."

Max reached into the cabinet for a plate. Harrison allowed it. "So it's true," he said. "You're one of Santa's elves."

"Is there any other kind?" George wondered, supervising Max's selection of pizza slice. "Don't be shy, flappy."

"Aren't there other types of elves?" Harrison asked. He assumed there were.

"I don't know," George responded impatiently. "*Are* there? The only elves I know live up north."

Max returned with the plate of pizza and stood in front of George. "Oh man, look at that," she said, "Georgie like-y." She leaned forward to take a bite, mouth agape. Max awkwardly held out the plate with the tip of the slice hanging off the edge, but Harrison suddenly pulled the plate back.

"Aw, come on, man! I'm hungry!" George was more annoyed than desperate.

"What did you mean when you said you were at the right house?" Harrison stared at George. George stared back. Neither blinked.

"Can I have a bite first?" George asked nicely.

Harrison shook his head *no*.

"Okay.... Can I have a bite...after?" George lifted her eyebrows, figuring there was a little room for negotiation.

"Only one way to find out," Harrison reasoned. "Tell us why you're here."

"Fine. I am here to retrieve some paperwork." She opened her mouth and leaned forward for a bite. Harrison still had his hand on the plate, keeping it at a distance.

"What paperwork?"

"Bite first," George demanded.

Harrison took the plate from Max and walked over to the trash can. He stepped on the foot-pedal that opened the lid and dangled the pizza over the trash.

"Nononono!" George pleaded. "I'll talk, I'll talk!" She composed herself, trying to remain dignified. "I'm here to retrieve an extremely sensitive document for the BMOC."

"The BMOC?" Max wondered.

"Yeah, the BMOC." George's impatience returned. "You know, the BMOC: the Big Man on Christmas. Big Red. The Man with the Beard. Saint Nick-a-doo. Nicky Chub Chubs. Ole Sandy Pants?" Her eyes panned back and forth between Harrison and Max. "That was enough, right? Do you still need me to say it? That I'm here to pick up some paperwork for Santa Claus?" The boys' silence annoyed her.

"Was it a travel itinerary?" Max offered. Harrison elbowed Max in the arm again. There was no reason Max needed to offer that information to their prisoner.

George focused on Max, sizing him up, wondering how much of an ally he could be for her. But she played it cool. "I don't know what you think you've seen," she stated, "but if you are in possession of something that could have similarities to what might look like a printed travel itinerary, then it would be wise to hand it over to me immediately."

Harrison stepped toward George, cool as a frozen cucumber. He leaned down, eye-level with his captive elf. "We don't know what you're talking about."

George turned her head and offered a side-eyed glance. She smiled, playing along. *"Exactly,"* she stated with a wink.

"Yeah we do, Harrison," Max broke cover. "You found it on the roof."

"Bingo." George smiled at Max. She had found her information sieve. The kid couldn't keep a secret if the world depended on it.

"Max, just please be quiet," Harrison demanded.

"Look pal," George said impatiently, "I've got a bit of a short temper. In fact, the Big Man thinks I'm something of a misfit elf and apparently it's gotten in the way of my toy making abilities. And fine, maybe it has, and maybe I deserve to be thrown off the toyline even though I couldn't care less about the toyline because I just wanna work in electronics and develop apps for the rest of my life, okay, and maybe I deserve this little punishment for almost ruining Christmas for the entire world, blah, blah, but if I don't return home with that itinerary then I'm pretty much in for another year off the toyline. And for an elf to not be making Christmas presents, it's like not being an elf at all. Just ask those shelf elfs."

Harrison leaned back on his heels. It was a lot of information to absorb, but it didn't answer the main question. "Why does Santa care about some dumb travel itinerary so much?"

George stared at Harrison, contemplating whether to reveal what some would consider one of the greatest unknowns about the North Pole's most famous resident. "Because..." she started, hesitating slightly. "Because Mr. Ho-Ho-Ho likes to spend his vacation with Mrs. Ho-Ho-Ho in a little resort town in Florida—undisturbed, mind you—and since Mr. Forgetful Claus requires an actual print-out of his travel plans, and because he happened to whip out his Droid to send a text to dear Mrs. Claus on *your* roof, accidentally dropping his hard copy travel itinerary in the process and can't have the details of his private vacation getting into the wrong hands and plastered all over the Internet, he forces the misfit elf to cancel her much anticipated trip to Ibiza to clean up his mess."

Harrison nodded confidently, as if he'd known all along. Max raised his eyebrows as the truth finally dawned on him.

"OH MY GOSH!" he yelled. "Harrison, you were right! *Dad* was right!"

George's eyes whipped to Max. "Right about what? What was Dad right about? Dad who?"

Harrison smiled. He pulled the folded travel itinerary from his pocket. "It's true then," he said, matter-of-fact. "Santa goes on vacation after Christmas."

"Uh, yeah. You're holding the stupid itinerary right there in your hands."

"Which means this is day one of Naughty Week," Harrison confirmed.

George looked at Harrison, then at Max, then back at Harrison. Both had the same sly grin on their faces. George closed her eyes and raised her eyebrows, backpedaling. "I cannot confirm or deny the existence of such a week."

"This is amazing! It's Naughty Week! It's real! We can do whatever we want!" Max could not contain himself. His hair fell over his eyes as he smiled wide.

"Take it easy there, flappy," George stated.

"Let's do something crazy! What should we do?" It was an information sugar bomb, and Max's fuse was lit.

George cleared her throat. "As the only adult here, I am going on record as advising against any crazy-going. In my experience, it only leads to trouble."

The tone of her voice suggested there might have been something in her recent history that she was referring to. Harrison sensed it, but he wanted to stick to the task at hand.

"It's Naughty Week," he stated. "We can do anything we want. What could possibly go wrong?"

12

NAUGHTY WEEK: DAY 1

"Look here," George lowered her voice. Her size and her jolly nature betrayed the serious attitude she attempted to convey. "You boys play with fire," she warned, "you're gonna get burned."

Unable to contain himself, Max grabbed a plate off the kitchen counter and slammed it to the floor. SMASH!

"HA HA," he celebrated.

"Nice one," Harrison commended.

Harrison slipped George's lonely slice of pizza off the plate and onto the kitchen table, then threw the plate down to the ground. SMASH!

"You two are animals," George stated. "Those plates don't clean up themselves, you know. And I kinda don't appreciate you throwing my slice on the table like that. Have a little respect." She eyed the slice of pizza, which dangled pathetically over the edge of the table.

"What else, what else?" Harrison scanned the kitchen.

"I don't know! Think!" There was an urgency to Max's voice that Harrison appreciated. The boys searched the cabinets for ideas as George shimmied her chair over to the kitchen table, getting close enough to nibble the slice of pizza hanging over the edge.

"We could prank call teachers from school." Harrison suggested. He knew it was kind of lame, but he was just spit-balling.

"Borrrrr-ring," George taunted.

"We could toilet paper someone's house."

"Lame," George said.

A light bulb suddenly shined over Max's head. "I know," he said, "we can chuck yellow snowballs at cars!"

"Gross!" George shut it down, though there was something innately creative about the suggestion. Throwing snowballs at cars was all too ordinary. Throwing *yellow* snowballs at cars did absolutely suggest a certain naughtiness appropriate for Naughty Week.

"We gotta think big," Harrison proposed. "We gotta make the most of our situation."

He propped himself up on the kitchen counter, set his elbow on his thigh and his chin on his fist. He understood that he faced incredible opportunity, and he didn't want to squander it like the time he sold the most magazine subscriptions in fourth grade. The grand prize for each class was a ride in a limousine and a pizza party. Harrison had never ridden in a limo, and it sounded so luxurious and awesome that he just had to win. He went in with a classmate, an entrepreneurial orange-haired kid named Emmett. They made a deal: Harrison would receive credit and earn points toward the grand prize limousine ride for every sale they made, and Emmett would receive the tickets on the indi-vidual sales, which could be traded in for things like candy, toys, and gift cards.

Every day they went door-to-door in the neighborhood. They fanned out until they hit every house on every street in a half-mile radius. If someone wasn't home after school, they would mark that house on a map and return on a Saturday or Sunday. They were committed young sales professionals, and their conversion rate was through the roof.

When the campaign ended, Harrison had earned the limousine ride. The limo picked up all of the winners after school on a Friday. Inside the limo, it was cramped. Harrison wanted to open the sunroof, but he was told not to touch any of the buttons. A few sodas laid on ice, and small bags of chips sat in a clear plastic bowl. The limo drove them the twenty minutes to Continental Pizza, and they had their pizza party. Then the limo drove them back to school. For the hard work Harrison put into selling all of those magazine subscriptions, the reward fell short. Meanwhile, Emmett collected about $150 in gift cards.

It was Harrison's first official Naughty Week, and he wanted it to be great. George sensed his inner conflict. She shook her head, disappointed.

"Look," she said, "if you boys truly want to commit to this thing, I may be willing to get the ball rolling."

"How so?" Harrison wondered.

"I can help, but we gotta make a deal."

George had Harrison and Max's full attention. Harrison hopped down from the kitchen counter and folded his arms across his chest. "Okay. I'm listening."

"First, you untie me," George squirmed in her bungee cord bindings. "Then I eat as much pizza as I want. Those two deal points are non-negotiable."

Harrison looked at Max. They both wondered where she was going with this.

"Then and only then," George continued, "I'll help you do your naughty thing."

Harrison considered her offer. "How do we know you won't run away?"

George looked at Harrison with the seriousness of a librarian. "Have you ever had North Pole pizza? North Pole pizza is the worst. It tastes like polar bear fur, only chewier." The sincerity of her tone seemed authentic. She was serious about pizza, but did that convince the boys enough to untie her? "Also," she went on, "this whole naughty deal sounds like it could be a hoot, *especially* with my help. But when we're done here—and this is the main thing—you've gotta hand over that itinerary."

Harrison studied George's eyes. Maybe she *could* help them have an awesome Naughty Week. And what if she did just run away? It doesn't change the fact that Harrison and Max would be spending the next seven days going absolutely bonkers. For Harrison, it was worth taking the deal.

"Okay," Harrison stated, "it's a deal." He nodded at Max, and Max started unclasping the bungee cords.

"You need to understand something first," George said, shifting her tiny body as she became free. "There are rules." The bungee cords dropped to the kitchen tile. George hopped off the chair and went directly for the pizza boxes.

"Rules?" Harrison raised his eyebrows.

"I can give you pretty much whatever you want," George · started. "But *only* what my two little hands and a tiny sack of Christmas dust can make."

George tossed a maroon velvet bag no larger than a lacrosse ball onto the table and opened one of the pizza boxes.

"Christmas dust?" Max had never heard of such a thing. He reached for the little velvet bag, and George slapped his hand away.

"Don't ever touch my Christmas dust. This stuff is extremely unstable and should only be handled by professional elves."

"We can ask for anything?" Harrison wondered.

"Don't ask for cash or pets," George warned. "Animals must come from Granny or Gramps or Mom and Dad, and the World

Trade Organization has a strict no-cash policy on Christmas. Santa takes this very seriously."

George stacked four large slices of pepperoni pizza, one on top of the other. "And please don't ask for world peace because North Polians simply don't get involved in politics." She moved to the refrigerator and found the green canister of grated parmesan. She dumped it onto her quadruple-decker pizza stack.

"I don't perform medical miracles *or* report card miracles," she continued. "If you're failing school, then you're more than likely on the naughty list anyway, so..."

Harrison watched her as she set her plate on the kitchen table and hopped onto a chair. "So you're like a genie?" he asked.

"Trust me," she said, "if I could sleep undisturbed for thousands of years in a tiny little lamp, I should be so lucky."

Her jaw opened wide, and she took a large bite out of the pizza stack. "So," she said with a mouthful, "what do you maniacs wanna do first?"

13

THE INVISIBLE ALL-TERRAIN SUPER POWER JET MOBILE

Harrison, Max, and George stood in the backyard in a triangular huddle. Harrison and Max were dressed warmly in mismatched clothing. George didn't seem cold. For her, this hardly compared to North Pole temperatures.

"Well?" Harrison asked expectantly. He and Max smiled wide-eyed with anticipation.

George looked confused. "I don't know even know what that is. Did you just make that up?"

"Yeah," Harrison replied. "So what?"

"If it doesn't exist, and if I have nothing to base it on, then I can't make it. And to be honest, what you're asking for doesn't really sound like a toy."

"I thought elves could make anything," Harrison challenged. "Or does that just apply to *upstanding* elves?"

"Oh no, you didn't just go there," George took the bait. "Stand back, flappy. Watch yourselves."

George stepped to the middle of the yard. The frozen snow crunched softly beneath her little feet. She removed her maroon sack of Christmas dust and poured a pinch in her hand.

"Okay, let's see... One, uh, super all invisible..." she looked at Harrison. "What the heck is it?"

"Invisible All-Terrain Super Power Jet Mobile!" Harrison's voice echoed in the neighborhood.

"Okay," George stated. "One Invisible All-Terrain Super Power Jet Mobile coming right up." She lifted her hand into the air, spiked the Christmas dust onto the ground, and POOF!

There was a short, white flash and a cloud of vapor and...it appeared. Just like that, it appeared. A beautiful, shiny, cherry red Invisible All-Terrain Super Power Jet Mobile. Harrison and Max shielded their eyes, but only for the briefest of moments. When their eyes adjusted and they saw what stood before them, they were gobsmacked.

"Whoa!"

"Awesome!"

George approached the jet mobile like a rockabilly mechanic fresh from the depths of a garage. From her peacoat she produced an oily blue rag and wiped her hands.

"I based the design on the Vespa, if a Vespa had streamlined wings, jet propulsion, and a cloaking device." A certain pride overtook her voice. "It's all-terrain, like you asked, so snow, mud, sea, land, air, you name it. Gets a thousand miles to the gallon...*of water*." She smiled, especially proud of that feature. "Seatbelts are tough on a vehicle like this, so once she's fired up the gravity seat will be activated to keep you monkeys locked on. The seat fits three comfortably. Faux-leather, of course, because why remove an innocent creature from this world just to amuse you punks? Anyway, I think the chrome trim is a nice touch, and the red, well...everything looks better in red, don't you agree?"

For the first time in her long career on the toyline, George produced something strictly from her imagination. Sure, Harrison made the request, but there was nothing like an Invisible All-Terrain Super Power Jet Mobile in the world. There were rules about invention at the North Pole, and George broke about a dozen of them in less time than it takes to pop a bag popcorn in the microwave. Invisibility? That's a big no-no. Water-powered? If it hadn't been invented in the lower Earth, then it can't be done in the North Pole. Jet propelled and all-terrain? Santa might have had something to say about giving kids a flying machine. And the gravity seat? George has had that one up her sleeve since Elon Musk launched SpaceX.

George had a ton of ideas but was never able to flex her imagination. She had ideas on how to improve bicycles, skateboards, standard wooden building blocks and Lincoln Logs, sports equipment, and action figures. But would Santa listen to her ideas? No way. Ever heard of Magna-Tiles? George came up with that same idea in the 1980s, but the BMOC wouldn't let her execute the concept. And then in 1992 a Japanese math teacher invented geometric tiles that formed together using magnets to help his students learn about shapes. George wasn't angry, she didn't want credit. She was just happy her brilliant idea could now be shipped off the toyline.

Harrison and Max circled the jet mobile. They had never seen anything like it. "So how does it get invisible?" Harrison wondered.

George furrowed her eyebrows, annoyed. She pointed to the sleek, minimalist dashboard above the steering console. "Push the invisibility button, genius."

"How fast does it go?" Max blurted.

George smiled knowingly. "Oh, she's fast enough for you, flappy." Then she nodded toward the jet mobile. "Hop on, let's take her for a spin."

Harrison and Max jumped into the long leather seat. Harrison held onto the handle bars, and Max wrapped his arms around Harrison's waist. George whipped out a small, handheld remote control and pressed the start button. The jet mobile roared to life, and the gravity seat pulled Harrison and Max tightly to the vehicle. The force was strong enough that Max let go of Harrison to gain balance, but by doing so he overcompensated and nearly fell off the jet mobile. But the gravity seat kept his bottom firmly on the faux-leather. George again smiled at her handywork.

"Back up, kiddo," she said to Harrison, approaching the jet mobile. "I'm driving."

"I want to drive," Harrison whined. Of course he wanted to drive. Who wouldn't want to drive this thing?

"When *you* create an Invisible All-Terrain Super Power Jet Mobile, then you can drive first." Harrison relented, sliding back on the seat.

George hopped on and reached into her pocket. She took a small pinch of Christmas dust and flung it at Max's head, and a blue bike helmet appeared fitted over his bushy hair. George took another pinch and flung it at Harrison's head, and a red bike helmet appeared. Another pinch, and she flung it on her own head. A silver hockey helmet with a high impact-resistant clear plastic visor appeared on her small head. Stenciled into the side: *George*. Harrison and Max looked on enviously.

"Hang on, boys." George revved the jet mobile's engine. She advanced them forward, circling around the backyard. The all-weather eighteen-inch tires cut through the snow and ice with ease. They rode down the side of the house to the driveway and rolled out to the sidewalk. George looked both ways before pulling into the street.

"Is this it?" Harrison wondered, unimpressed.

"I thought you said it was fast!" Max complained.

They moved at a mediocre three miles per hour. If Mrs. Sylvester down the street had been on her late afternoon jog, she would've been able to run circles around them.

"Come on, faster!" Max demanded.

"Fine." George accelerated to about five miles per hour and drove the jet mobile toward the cul-de-sac.

"Oh, now we're really moving," Harrison uttered sarcastically. He let go of George. Max let go of Harrison. They let their arms dangle by their sides as they made the wide turn, very slowly, around the cul-de-sac.

George could feel their disappointment. "You know," she stated, "when you requested this little Invisible All-Terrain Super Power Jet Mobile, you didn't actually specify how fast you wanted it to go." She made a good point. Harrison kicked himself. How could he leave out a detail like that?

"That said," George continued, "Do you think *I'd* invent something that couldn't do better than a golf cart?" The jet mobile came to a stop in the middle of the cul-de-sac. She turned around to look at the boys as the vehicle idled. Harrison and Max weren't sure what she meant by that. Harrison just shrugged.

Finally, George flipped a few switches and revved the accelerator, and the jet mobile suddenly hovered in place about a meter off the ground.

"Whoa!" Max shouted.

The jet mobile lifted farther into the air. In the house behind them, Mr. and Mrs. Holiday's German shepherd, Gertie, started barking. Max squeezed his arms tighter around Harrison's body.

"Don't worry back there." George sensed the boys' nervousness. She lifted her fist and pointed her thumb down toward the seat. "Gravity seats. This may be bootleg technology, but you're not going *anywhere*."

Suddenly, the jet mobile blasted forward, leaving a trail of effervescent white light.

"YEEEEEEEAAAAAAAAAAHHHHHHHH!!!"

The jet mobile went from zero to 120 miles per hour in a split second. George navigated the jet mobile over the trees and rooftops, above telephone wires and street lamps, higher into the sky.

"This is sweeeeeet!" Harrison shouted.

"Whoooooooaaaaaaa!" Max yelled.

"What's that?!" George asked over the noise of the wind rushing past. "You want to go *faster*?!" She revved the engine and accelerated them to 140 miles per hour.

"Where are we going?!" Harrison shouted.

"I don't know," George said. "North maybe?"

The dense neighborhoods below them disappeared in an instant. They flew above a less populated area—fewer houses, fewer street lights, more trees and forests. It had only been a short time, but Harrison thought they could be as far as Pennsylvania by now.

"I'm gonna baaaaaaarf!" Max roared with delight.

"This is nothing!" George yelled over her shoulder. "We haven't even tried the nitro boosters." She lifted a small panel on the dash, revealing the nitro booster button. Harrison and Max's eyes grew wide.

Nitro boosters? Harrison wondered. They'd be in New York before long.

"Do it! Do it!" he yelled. He had never gone this fast in his life. It was exhilarating and scary all at once.

George held up her pointer finger, then slowly brought it down to the nitro booster button. She paused, hovering her finger just above the button.

"Flappy?" she called back to Max. "You good back there?"

"Do it!" he hollered.

George smiled, then pressed the nitro booster button, and the jet mobile shot forward to 160 miles per hour.

"AAAAAAAAAAAAAHHHHHHH!!!"

14

JACK

In the back corner of a CVS parking lot on the outskirts of Potomac, Maryland, a thirty-nine-foot 1999 turbo diesel Bounder rested against the plowed snow in the cold night, bothering no one. The recreational vehicle's headlights blinked on, and the engine roared to life. The Bounder slowly creeped its way out of the parking lot onto Democracy Boulevard toward Potomac.

The RV rolled down the road in the right lane, careful to remain under the speed limit as it drove into an unassuming Potomac neighborhood, where the average home stood at five-thousand square feet and held five or more bedrooms. The Bounder bounded down a quiet section of River Falls Drive, quite the fish out of water in these parts. At the top of the street, the RV's headlights suddenly cut off. It coasted down the pavement and rolled to a stop.

After a minute, the door opened and a man hopped out. He was a tall man, a handsome man of slim stature, and he wore a faded Santa costume.

He moved around the RV to the side door and pulled on the square metal lever to open it. He reached inside and unloaded an oversized duffel bag and a roller suitcase, both empty. He slipped the shoulder strap of the duffel onto his shoulder and raised the handle on the roller suitcase. He reached back into the Bounder and removed a plastic cat carrier, and the critter inside let out an innocent "Meow."

Given the Santa suit and the cat, it would have been relatively obvious who this gentleman was had anyone been paying attention to the local news. His name was Jack Dolan, but this week he was better known for his alias, the Santa Claws Cat Burglar.

Jack eyed a home isolated among the evergreen trees. The porch light shined, but the house otherwise stood dark. He headed up the long, empty driveway toward the backyard, where an oblong-shaped pool sat empty and covered for winter. A layer of snow weighed down the vinyl covering like a fluffy white cat resting in a blue hammock.

At the end of the pool deck was a back door with nine small panes of glass. Jack parked the roller suitcase and cat carrier, and with little hesitation—CRASH—broke the bottom left glass pane.

An alarm sounded—EEP EEP EEP!—blaring through the house.

Jack reached inside and unlocked the door, then moseyed to a home security wall panel. He tapped a few numbers, and the high-pitched alarm went silent. He smiled to himself, crediting his time at Whipperwill Home Security for being able to work under pressure so well and hacking home alarm systems so easily. He would still be working there, but he felt his supervisor had overlooked him for the systems manager promotion he knew he deserved, and he resented not being awarded the position due to what the human resources director cited was an inability to work well with his peers.

He returned to the back door, grabbed the empty roller suitcase and cat carrier, and headed inside to liberate the home of any and all valuables, and to also liberate the mange-ridden twelve-year-old tabby-mix he acquired from the Rockville Animal Shelter earlier that morning.

15

THE MOM PROBLEM

A thick blanket of snow covered the high mountains in Vail. The sun had by now dropped below the horizon, spreading an orange glow through the floor-to-ceiling glass panes of Mom and Dale's tawdry ski chalet.

In the kitchen, Mom sliced cheese on a cutting board, transferring bite-sized chunks to a platter where apple slices and grapes had already been prepared. Mom eyed her cell phone beside the platter. She wanted to call and check on her boys but had resisted since her plane landed. *They're in good hands*, she told herself.

Dale trotted downstairs fresh from a shower in a plush white bathrobe that matched the plush white furniture and white carpeting. Mom thought of Harrison and Max and how the white couch and white carpet would have been stained with fruit juice or chocolate by now.

"Ooooh, cheese," Dale sang. "Lovely." Dale was a bit cheesy himself, but Mom didn't mind it so much.

"I feel like I can finally relax," she said. "No kids for one week. I should cherish every minute."

Dale circled behind Mom and wrapped his arms around her. She leaned her head back onto his chest. These two really liked each other.

"I do miss 'em, though," she said, hoping no one would hear.

"Of course you do. They're your boys." Dale spun her around to face him. "Why not give them a call?"

"No, I don't want to be *that* mom," she resisted.

"You mean the kind of mom that loves and misses her children? Lord no, please don't be that mom." Dale's dry sense of humor made Mom smile. "Fine. If you want to stay strong and not be *that mom*, then call them later, just to say goodnight."

Mom turned back around to finish the cheese platter. "The thing is," she started, "if I do that, then I might feel compelled to call them every night, and then they will have succeeded in breaking me down during *my* vacation, and I might resent them for that."

"You make a good point," Dale said. "But they are your children, and I know you miss them." Dale was a good guy. It was hard to deny. He broke a nibble of cheese off the cheese platter and fed it to her.

"The boys are in good, capable hands," Mom reassured herself for the millionth time. "They don't need their mother coddling them." She broke off a piece of cheese and fed it to Dale, then kissed him on the cheek. "One call, just to say goodnight." She grabbed her phone and hurried into the living room.

16

YADDA YADDA GRANDMA

Harrison, Max, and George sat around the kitchen table, red-faced from their high-speed adventure. They munched on room-temperature pizza and shared soda straight out of a two-liter bottle. After the thrill of traveling upward of two-hundred miles per hour, trading germs was the least of Harrison and Max's worries. Their posture stood a little straighter, their chins perched a little higher. They felt invincible.

"I think we might have crossed into New York," Harrison mused.

"I'll have the GPS working by sunup," George assured, quietly kicking herself for forgetting something as basic as a global positioning system. It was 2012, she thought. Even furniture has GPS.

Max stuffed half a slice of pizza into his mouth and chewed widely. He shook the hair out of his eyes. "That was awesome," he uttered, spitting bits of crust. "Let's go again!"

"Oh no," George said, not wanting to stare Max's great big mouthful of food directly in the eye. "Now we eat pizza. And then it's nigh-nigh for Georgie. There's nothing like a good night's sleep with a belly full of pepperoni."

"You know what would be awesome?" Max wondered. "If we got, like, a helmet cam. A video camera attached to our heads. Can you make that?"

George eyed Max. She appreciated his eagerness. "Take it easy. There's only so much Christmas dust," she warned. And it was true. George and the other elves on the toyline were only issued about one measuring cup full of X-MA5, a.k.a. Christmas dust. A little goes a long way, but there wasn't enough Christmas dust in the whole world to satisfy an eight year old's hunger for more stuff.

"Besides," George continued, still preoccupied with her pizza. "Do you really want video evidence of these little shenanigans getting back to Jolly Old Saint Roly-Poly?"

George had made a great point, and Harrison, who had been drumming up plans for Naughty Week Day Two in his imagination, finally piped up. "No way. No pictures. No video." He was firm and direct.

George smiled at Harrison. "Vegas rules," she stated. "I like it."

Suddenly the phone rang. It was one of those archaic landline portable deals mounted to the kitchen wall that sounded like a cell phone ringing underwater any time someone called.

Before Harrison could stop him, Max picked it up.

"Hello?"

"Hi hon, it's Mom."

Max looked directly at Harrison, who knew instantly who was on the other end. Harrison slumped at Max's novice mistake. The rules of Naughty Week had yet to be written, but somewhere at the top of the list should be: *When left on one's own, never ever ever EVER answer the phone because it's probably your mom.*

"Max?" Mom asked. Max's mouth was agape and noiseless, as if someone had reached down his throat and squeezed his vocal cords.

Seated by the fire in the living room of the ski chalet, Mom adjusted the position of her body to give her better phone reception. "Max, can you hear me?"

Harrison grabbed the phone out of Max's hand. "Mom, hi, it's Harrison."

"Hey, love, how's everything going?"

"Fine," Harrison responded quickly. Maybe a little too quickly.

"Are you sure?" Mom prodded. Moms have the ability to know when something is not quite right, especially when it comes to their kids.

"Yeah, we're here eating pizza. With Grandma," Harrison lied. "She's right here. With us."

"Good," Mom said. "Well, I'll let you get back to dinner. Put Grandma on."

Harrison's eyes widened. Why couldn't he have thought up a better lie? He could have said she was in the shower, or on the other line with Stanley, or shoveling snow outside. "Okay. Um, hold please."

Harrison tapped the mute button on the receiver and refocused his anger on Max. "Idiot!" he yelled. "She wants to talk to Grandma. We're so busted!"

"Sorry! I wasn't thinking!" Max whined. "I don't wanna go to Mrs. Klopek's house. Quick, do something!"

The gears in Harrison's mind churned. He was at a critical Naughty Week crossroads. He would either need to come clean to Mom, which would mean the end of Naughty Week after only a few hours, or he could find a solution to his problem clever enough to defy the one person that for all ten years of his life could never be defied.

Memories flooded Harrison's brain of all of the times Mom caught him in a lie. The time he ate a whole sleeve of Girl Scout Thin Mints before dinner. The time he took five dollars from Mom's purse. The time his friend Bobby slept over and they stayed up late and watched *Saw VII* on HBO. The time he dropped Max's prized Discovery Kids Bilingual Teach and Talk Tablet down the stairs. Mom busted him every time.

Harrison had a brief moment of regret, remembering how much Max loved that Teach and Talk Tablet. After Harrison dropped it down the stairs, he snuck it back into their bedroom and placed it under Max's bed. When Max found it, it wouldn't turn on. He changed the batteries, but still nothing. Max was so sad. After observing the scratches on the plastic corners of the device, Mom suspected something had happened, and that Harrison might have known something about it. She knew how jealous Harrison was when Max received it from Grandma for his birthday. Harrison kept the lie going for three days before the guilt was just too much. He finally owned up, apologized to Max, and came clean to Mom. She grounded him for a week.

Harrison snapped back to reality, still holding the phone. He looked at Max, then at George, and then he suddenly realized he had an ace up his sleeve.

"George!" he ordered. "Make me something like a Teach and Talk Tablet with a grandma-sounding voice. Quick!"

George narrowed her eyes. She knew what he was after but didn't much like the demand. "Did I hear a 'please' in there?" she asked calmly.

"Please, please, pretty please can you make us a grandma voice Teach and Talk Tablet?! And can you please please hurry?!"

George took a bite of pizza. Half a pepperoni dangled from her tiny lips. "Teach and Talk Tablet? What is this, 1998? I can do better than a Teach and Talk." She reached her greasy hand outward. "You got a smartphone? An iPod Touch?"

Harrison quickly handed over his iPod Touch. George removed a white cable from her pocket and connected it from Harrison's iPod to her own iPhone. She opened an app on her phone and quickly tapped a few instructions. She reached into another pocket and pulled out the little sack of Christmas dust. She eyed Harrison and Max insecurely and sprinkled some over her iPhone.

"I can do this without the Christmas dust, but my equipment is back at the Pole." Her iPhone pulsed a white light, which traveled through the cable to the iPod Touch. "Here," George said as she disconnected the iPod and handed it back to Harrison. "Grandma voice app."

Harrison unlocked the device and found the new app. The icon was a cartoonish looking grandmother, and the app was called "Yadda Yadda Grandma."

"You made this?" Harrison's mind was blown.

"Yeah I made it. Where do you think apps come from?" George hopped down from the counter. "I'll be in my office." She grabbed a Harry & David catalogue and headed for the bathroom.

Harrison quickly unmuted the house phone and placed it on speakerphone. "Mom, sorry. Here's Grandma."

"Love you!" Mom shouted from Vail.

Harrison loaded the Yadda Yadda Grandma app and typed something in. He looked at Max, thinking, *Here goes nothing.*

"Hello, daughter," the Grandma robot voice said. Max's eyes widened. It sounded uncannily like Grandma. But because the voice was being processed through a phone, it was impossible to tell it came from an app. Harrison just needed to keep the conversation convincing.

"Hello, mother," Mom said. "How's everything going?"

Harrison typed furiously. "Fine... How are you?"

"Good. Things are...great, actually. Dale is just...such a great guy. I think I lucked out."

Harrison looked at Max and rolled his eyes.

"Anyway," Mom continued, "I take it you found the cash I left?"

Harrison typed quickly, "Yes... Is there any more money... hidden in the house?"

Max slapped Harrison's arm. *"What are you doing?"*

"Uh, no," Mom said, "but if you need to buy anything, I can reimburse you."

Harrison typed: "Never mind."

"Okay, well, have fun this week. Call me anytime." Harrison could hear a tinge of heartache in Mom's voice. He could tell Mom missed them.

Harrison typed "goodbye" and hung up the phone. "That was close," he said with a sigh of relief.

"That Grandma app voice sounded just like Grandma!" Max still couldn't believe it.

A flush sounded from the other room. George entered, tossing the Harry & David catalogue onto the counter. "The downstairs bathroom is closed until further notice," she said. "So how'd it go with Mom?"

"Amazing," Harrison said. "How did you get it to sound just like Grandma?"

George stared at Harrison. "I am a legit app developer. I've got ideas for apps that would blow your mind, and the training to execute. Trouble is, I'm not allowed to develop them because most of the technology that I need to employ has not yet been invented."

"Also the Christmas dust is like magic, right?" Max piped in.

George looked at Max dismissively. "The Christmas dust just speeds things along, that's all."

"So what should we do next?" Harrison wondered.

"You boys can do whatever you like. I'm turning in. It's gonna be a loooooong week." George headed upstairs for bed as Harrison and Max looked at each other, smiling wide. It was the first night of Naughty Week. There was absolutely no way they were going to bed this early.

17

NAUGHTY WEEK: NIGHT 1

J ack navigated the 1999 Bounder across the backroads of suburban Maryland. He used his turn indicator to switch lanes, extra careful to obey all traffic laws because just behind him, inside the RV, sat three homes' worth of valuables. He had six flat screen TVs, stereo equipment, video game consoles, boxes of jewelry, fancy silverware, leather jackets and fur coats, and a toaster oven.

He had a rule about what he took. He only stole things that could easily be replaced. If a piece of jewelry looked like it might have been a family heirloom, he left it behind. He didn't take computer equipment either. What if there was something on there that couldn't be replaced? Family photos? A half-finished novel? A dissertation? A high school senior's admissions letter? Jack wouldn't be able to live with himself if it meant an ambitious seventeen year old couldn't go to the college of her dreams. Besides, the average Montgomery County family home held no shortage of valuables. He had boosted enough stuff to open his own pawn shop.

The RV crossed over a pothole with a THUD. *Meow meow*

meow. Jack also had possession of five cats in cat carriers. If a police officer pulled him over, the stolen goods would have raised plenty of suspicions, but the five random cats in cat carriers stolen from animal shelters would seal his fate. How could he possibly deny being the Santa Claws Cat Burglar?

It was worth the risk, he mused. These cats needed good homes. The well-off families he stole from could certainly afford to fall in love and care for an animal in need. Not only had he saved the lives of these cats, but he also brought priceless joy into households that may otherwise not know the joy of caring for a domestic pet. Jack had the remarkable ability to justify things in his mind.

The RV rolled over a rough patch on the pavement. *Meow meow meow.* Jack eyed the rearview mirror. The little creatures were getting hungry. He would need to pull over soon and feed them their evening meal of half dry food and half wet food. He had plenty of food. Earlier in the day, he pawned one of the smaller flat screens for sixty-five dollars. He spent forty-five dollars on cat food, litter, and a few more little aluminum litter boxes to place inside of each cat carrier. With the rest of the money he bought two five-dollar footlongs from Subway and a large soda. He loved the five-dollar footlong song. He couldn't nibble on his spicy Italian sandwich without singing to himself, *"Five...five...five-dollar foot-loooooooooong."* Classic, he thought.

Meow. Jack couldn't take it anymore. The poor little critters needed to eat. He flipped on his right indicator light and turned into a quiet neighborhood on a street that ended in a cul-de-sac. He drove halfway down the block and pulled over. The street was dark and quiet and unsuspecting.

He unbuckled his seat belt and worked his way to the back of the RV where the cat carriers were lined neatly in a row. He opened the door to each carrier, letting the cats move around and stretch their legs. He piled half a can of wet food into paper bowls, then poured dry food on top of each, and the cats eagerly hustled toward the sound of the kibbles.

Jack sat on the padded bench and watched the cats eat. He didn't feel inconvenienced by these mangy little animals. He felt lucky to have them. He scratched their heads as they ate, and then something caught his attention.

Across the street, a house stood wide awake. Every other house on the block was completely dark, and yet pretty much every light in this house burned bright. He moved for the side door of the Bounder and opened it. He could hear music and the low rumble of video game explosions. And then the sound of boys' laughter.

He checked the RV's digital clock. It was 3:39 a.m. Jack couldn't understand how children could be up this late, or how they could get away with playing video games so loud in the middle of the night.

It made him uncomfortable enough to want to get out of there. What if one of the neighbors called the police? He didn't want to chance being stuck on the block when the cops came to shut down that party or whatever was going on in there. He placed the cats back into the cat carriers and climbed into the driver's seat. He buckled his seat belt and started up the RV. As he pulled away, he eyed the house again. Something about that was awful curious to him.

18

NAUGHTY WEEK: DAY 2

George stood at the entryway of the living room, sipping from a cup of coffee, observing the mess of humanity heaped before her. Harrison slept face-down on the soda-stained floor. A video game controller tilted halfway off his hand. Around him, candy wrappers were strewn about, along with half a loaf of white bread with staling slices tumbling from the plastic bag. Max slept on the couch under an avalanche of pillows and empty soda bottles.

George looked at the clock above the TV. It was 8:47 a.m. Back in the North Pole, there was rare a day in which George climbed out of bed this early. She liked her sleep, but more importantly she didn't like her position on the toyline. She lacked motivation, and it showed. Now, for whatever reason, something about Harrison and Max gave her newfound purpose, as if she had a fresh assignment, a job that only she could do. She was wide awake and felt alive and motivated to start her day.

"Look at these guys," George said quietly to herself. "Couple'a little angels." She smiled and sipped her coffee, then set down her coffee mug on the TV cabinet and removed a pinch of Christmas dust. A soft POOF, and she was gripping a bullhorn.

BE-LOOP BE-LOOP BE-LOOP!!!

Harrison and Max jumped to attention, groggy but not wide awake.

"Rise and shine, greaseballs!" George announced into the bullhorn. "It's a beautiful day to be naughty!"

Max rubbed his crusty, half-closed eyes. "Five more minutes," he moaned.

"No! Wake up, wake up!" George drilled. "It's naughty time!"

19

THE SNOW PROBLEM

Max raised to his tiptoes, reached into the kitchen cabinet, and removed a cereal bowl. He moved to the kitchen table and set it down next to a spoon and a five-pound bag of holiday themed peanut M&Ms. He filled the cereal bowl with the red and green candy, uncapped a gallon of milk, and poured. As he started into his breakfast, Harrison reached for the peanut M&Ms and scooped a handful into the pitcher of a blender, which had already been prepared with whipped cream, chocolate sauce, cherry juice, peanut butter, and rainbow sprinkles. He locked the pitcher onto the blender and blended his morning "energy shake" on medium.

"So what's the plan, kiddos?" George asked. She held a fresh cup of coffee and grabbed a slice of pizza from the fridge with her free hand. She hip-checked the refrigerator door closed and sat across from Max at the kitchen table.

Harrison shut off the blender. "What about a snowmobile race?" He poured his shake into a cup.

"Awesome!" Max shouted, crunching on his peanut M&M cereal. "We'll need snowmobiles, though."

George looked at Harrison quizzically as she dipped her slice of pizza in her coffee. "Was the Invisible All-Terrain Super Power Jet Mobile not enough?"

"I've never been on a snowmobile," Harrison stated matter-of-factly.

George nodded, chewing her pizza. "It's like jet skiing in snow. But jet skiing is so much better. And faster. Snow machining—and that's what we call it up north, snow *machining*—that's like...meh."

"If you can't make a snowmobile, then just say so," Harrison taunted.

"Oh I can make a snow *machine*, that's not the issue." George tempered her annoyance. "But we've got a serious lack-of-snow problem. And the snow that's out there won't be out there for long, considering it's forty-two degrees and sunny."

Harrison and Max looked out the kitchen window. It was, in fact, a sunny, unseasonably warm day for the end of December. The back patio was wet, and there were now only patches of snow in the grass.

"The snow's melting." Max worried. "Fix it!"

George looked at Max dismissively. "As if I can control the weather."

"Well, do *something*." Max's petulance was too much for George to handle at this hour of the morning. She waded over to the coffee maker and topped herself off.

Harrison stared out the window, quietly thinking.

"Look, flappy," George said, sipping coffee, "a snow machine without snow ain't a snow machine. It's a very expensive lawn ornament."

Harrison finally blinked. He turned to George with an idea. "Three snow machines, please," he stated, as if nothing George just said meant anything to him.

"You hard of hearing, fella?" George wanted the snow machine conversation to end.

"But first, something else." Harrison grinned slyly and eyed Max, and Max mirrored Harrison's sly grin but didn't know why.

George raised her tiny eyebrows. "This oughta be good," she challenged.

Harrison had remembered the time he and Dad drove to White-tail for a skiing day trip. It was late January but it felt like spring. The digital thermometer above the rearview mirror in Dad's car read fifty-two degrees. Harrison knew it wasn't cold enough for the snow to stay packed and had some concern that they would arrive after two and a half hours of driving only to find a mountain of draining slush. That's when he learned about a ski resort's best friend: the industrial snowmaker. No matter how quickly the natural snow melted on a mountain, the resort could produce more at the switch of a button.

"One snowmaker, please," Harrison requested, careful to ask politely.

George squinted at Harrison and nearly opened her mouth to protest, but then something stopped her. Maybe it was Harrison's inventive way of problem solving. Maybe she simply missed the feeling of snow falling on her ears. Or maybe, just maybe, she wanted to feel the magnificent diesel-fueled grind of a snow machine in her hands. Whatever the case, without a word she snapped her fingers and marched out of the room.

Outside, George headed toward the empty cul-de-sac at the end of the street, buttoning up her pea coat. Harrison and Max hurried to pull on their winter jackets, gloves, and boots. They had only made it off the front stoop when POOF, an industrial-sized, mountain-blanketing snowmaker appeared in the cul-de-sac. Within seconds, snow came pouring like a blizzard out of its long, wide chute, and the block started accumulating cold, white powder.

Harrison and Max raced toward the falling snow when—POOF, POOF, POOF—three cherry red Polaris 850 PRO-RMK snow machines appeared in the middle of the snow-covered street. Two were regular-sized snowmobiles and one was an elf-sized snow *machine*. Harrison and Max stopped dead in their tracks as George scurried over from the snowmaker's controls.

"Should be good in a few minutes," she stated. She then pointed at the snow machines. "What do you think of the rides? I went with red again. Sorry, but everything looks better in red."

Harrison and Max were speechless. Never in their lives had they witnessed anything so extraordinary happen on their block. There was that one time Mom organized a bouncy castle for a Labor Day block party, but that didn't come close to the awesomeness delivered to them by a clever North Polian elf. Harrison knew it would only be a matter of time before Mrs. Klopek nosed her way into their business, but he didn't care. When would he ever get another chance to ride on a snow machine?

"Snow ramp'll be ready in about fifteen minutes," George announced, mounting her snow machine. "We gonna carve out some tracks or what?"

20

THE SNOW MACHINE RACE

W ithin thirty minutes, the entire block was blanketed in snow. Word had spread around the neighborhood that someone rented a snowmaker, and kids and parents came from all over to participate in the fun. Some grade schoolers made snow angels and sledded down the giant snow ramp in front of the Fulwell house. Moms and dads erected snowmen. Teenagers started a snowball fight. And everyone was impressed with the kids on snow machines.

Harrison raced around expertly, hopping over curbs, fishtailing down the sidewalk, and cruising over Mrs. Klopek's front lawn. He looked around and appreciated everyone having such a good time. He was proud of himself. This is what Naughty Week is all about. It's about sharing the fun and letting oneself go.

"Happy Naughty Week to all! And to all a naughty night!" he hollered as he met Max and George at the end of the street. Among the curious neighbors, a plain clothes man, seemingly out for an inconspicuous walk about the neighborhood, joined the horde. He was tall and trim and smelled of cat. It was Jack.

"Look out everyone!" Harrison announced as the snow

machines lined up at the end of the road. The dozens of specta-
tors moved to the sidewalk to form a long, straight raceway.
Harrison throttled his snow machine. Max pulled down his ski
goggles. George wiped her upper lip and pushed a giant wad of
Big League Chew bubble gum in her mouth.

"On your mark," Harrison yelled over the VROOM VROOM
of the snow machines. "Get set," VROOM VROOM VROOM.
"GO!"

The snow machines took off, accelerating at an impressively
high speed. The crowd cheered as Harrison, Max, and George
raced down Ambler Court. Harrison took the early lead, but then
Max pulled ahead. George was left in the dust on her miniature
snow machine.

Jack watched from the sidewalk, not exactly sure what he was
witnessing. He looked at the snowmaker, then at the snow
machines, then zeroed in on the kids racing on top of them. The
miniature snow machine George rode seemed odd but not that
out of the ordinary, considering everything was going miniature
these days. He looked at the house that was wide awake and
partying the night before, then back at Harrison and Max. Were
those the kids who lived there? And then he asked himself the
question that no one else in the neighborhood seemed to
wonder: how on earth could anyone afford to rent or own an
industrial-sized snowmaker or two-and-a-half snow machines?

A theory suddenly popped into Jack's head. *Maybe these people
won the lottery.* If that was the case, then it would explain how the
bedtime rules and quiet hours could afford to be abandoned. It
would also explain the giant snowmaker and the snow machines.
If they did, in fact, hit the lottery, he thought, then maybe it's
worth sticking around and gathering more information.

As Max neared the finish line, he could feel Harrison gaining
on him. Max tried to throttle faster, but he lost control and spun
out into a snowbank. Harrison pushed his snow machine to top

speeds and crossed the finish line faster than he could manage, heading directly for the snow ramp.

Harrison tried to throttle down, but he lost control. His snow machine's runners hit the ramp and up, up, up he went, launching off the ramp and soaring into the air. Holding onto the handle bars for dear life, his legs flung outward behind him.

"AAAAAAAAAAGGGGHHHH!!!"

In a split second he anticipated his trajectory, and it seemed he was heading directly over the house. But then what? Should he bail and hope his body would land on the roof and be slowed by the soft layer of powdery snow? Or should he hang on and let the snow machine break his fall? A thousand thoughts raced in his mind at once, and as he was halfway over the roof he pictured the sweet smiling face of his mother and then CRASH!

The snow machine slammed into the chimney. Harrison flipped over the handlebars like a fish jumping out of the water and zipped through the air with nothing more to break his fall than his own fragile limbs and noggin. He flailed his arms and legs as he ascended, soaring over the fence and toward the neighbor's backyard.

FLUMP! He disappeared in a big pile of powdery snow.

He rolled onto his back and pushed the snow off his body. His heart raced a mile a minute. He breathed short gasps of air. And he was smiling so wide it hurt. His cheeks were red from the snow melting off his face. He looked up at the blue sky and made a mental note to never forget the feeling of exhilaration he was experiencing in this very moment. Seizing little moments of joy and happiness was something Dad encouraged Harrison to do shortly after Dad received his diagnosis.

Ears still ringing from the ride, Harrison did not hear the pair of boots clomping toward him. Harrison looked up and found a tallish man standing directly between him and the bright winter sun. He squinted to focus better and could barely make out a gloved hand reaching down. Harrison reached for the open hand, and the man pulled him to his feet.

"That was awesome," Harrison mused. "Thanks, mister." He looked closer. "Do you live in the neighborhood?" There was something about the man's face that looked familiar, but Harrison couldn't pinpoint it.

"I'm visiting a friend a few streets over, and I was wondering what all the commotion was about. You got some major air there."

"Totally," Harrison concurred confidently.

"Too bad about the chimney. I think your snowmobile is totaled," the man stated, looking up toward Harrison's roof.

"It's a snow *machine*, and it doesn't matter. I can just ask for a new one."

"Wow. And just like that, you get a new one?" The man's tone had a hint of jealousy. Harrison nodded. "And your parents don't care that you smashed a perfectly good snow machine into their roof?"

"I can do anything I want," Harrison replied, not missing a beat. "It's Naughty Week."

"Naughty Week?" the man furrowed his right brow ever so curiously.

"The crazy thing is, most people don't even know it's Naughty Week," Harrison explained, brushing off the remaining snow.

"Naughty Week, huh?" the man wondered. "I'd like to hear more about this Naughty Week." He held out his hand to introduce himself. "I'm Jack."

Harrison looked Jack up and down, still unable to place where he had seen this man's face before. But he looked friendly enough.

"I'm Harrison. Pleased to meet you." Had Harrison known he was only days away from being an accomplice to a federal crime, he may not have so readily shook Jack's hand.

21

NAUGHTY WEEK, NEXT LEVEL

Max and George stood by the kitchen counter in damp clothes, rosy-nosed from the cold. They had removed all the fixings for ice cream sundaes and retrieved bowls from the pantry. George placed a slice of pizza in her bowl, added two scoops of vanilla, and then covered it with chocolate syrup.

"You really should try this," she said as she folded the pizza around the ice cream, brought it to her little mouth, and took as big a bite as she possibly could. Max watched, dumbfounded.

They heard the front door open and slam shut. "What's up, losers!" Harrison called from the foyer.

"In here, cheater!" Max called back, still stinging from the questionable loss to Harrison in the snow machine race.

Harrison entered. "I won, fair and square, so eat it."

"I'm not making you another snow machine," George stated firmly. "You need to learn respect for the machine. You don't control the machine. You harmonize with the machine. Got it?"

A few steps behind Harrison, Jack moseyed in, checking out the house as a cat burglar might be inclined to do.

"Whoa," George said, noticing Jack. "What's with the ugly, tall, horse-face guy?"

"This is Jack," Harrison introduced his new friend. "He's celebrating Naughty Week too."

"Aren't you a little old for Naughty Week, Jack?" There was something about Jack that didn't sit right with George, something in her gut that was telling her he couldn't be trusted.

"Naughty Week's like Slip 'N Slide," Jack said with a charming smile. "You're never too old." He leaned down to Harrison's ear. "What's with the elfish-looking short gal?"

"That's my brother, Max."

"Ha ha, very funny." Max self-consciously pushed the shock of hair out of his eyes.

"I'm cousin George," George stated with squint-filled suspicion. She had no intention of telling this stranger the truth about who she actually was. She sized up Jack from top to toe. "Say... you look familiar. You ever get up north? You know, Canada? Or even farther north than Canada?"

"Can't say that I have." Jack sized up George just the same.

"You sure about that, stretch?"

"Pretty sure, shorty."

"Don't call me shorty." George took another bite of her pizza sundae.

"Anyway," Harrison intervened, "Jack and I are planning something big. We're taking Naughty Week to the next level."

"Count me out," George announced. "I don't like the cut of this guy's jib."

"Yeah, like your jib's all that impressive," Jack responded.

George sniffed the air. "You smell like cat food."

"You smell like pepperoni." For whatever reason, the adults were behaving worse than the children. It made Harrison uncomfortable, but he shrugged it off. Misbehaving and Naughty Week go hand-in-hand, like peanut butter and chocolate.

"So what are you guys planning?" Max asked. He was curious but didn't want to sound too interested.

"The coolest thing ever!" Harrison smiled wide. He couldn't contain himself. "We're gonna rob a bank!"

Max's eyes widened. George dropped her pizza sundae. "Wow," she said, scooping up the food. "That is pretty stupid."

"You can't rob a bank," Max protested. "If you get caught stealing money from a bank, you'll be arrested and it'll go on your permanent record." Max didn't entirely possess the confidence to know what that meant, but he knew robbing a bank would be breaking the law.

Harrison rolled his eyes. "Dumby, we're not gonna actually steal any money. We just want to see if we can do it. Like we talked about."

"It's like an exhibition robbery," Jack reasoned. "Just for kicks. After all, it's Naughty Week, right? We should go crazy."

George dumped the mess of pizza and ice cream in the trash, wiped her hands on a towel, and folded her small arms across her chest. "No. Thank. You."

"I don't know, Harrison," Max worried, "I mean, can't we just hang out here and stay up late and eat junk food?"

"Fine. You're both out. Bye, dorks." Harrison and Jack exited.

George meandered over to the kitchen table where a box of pepperoni pizza sat open and a carton of ice cream slowly melted. "There's something about that guy I don't trust," she said. "Something that just dings my bell the wrong way, you know?"

Max shrugged. He had never met Jack before today, but George was right. It felt like he had seen Jack somewhere but just couldn't place it.

George stacked two slices of pizza on top of one another and dipped them into the softened ice cream like it was vanilla sauce. "Pass the hot fudge, flappy."

22

THE PLAN

Harrison and Jack sat on the floor of the basement. Between them stood a Lego-constructed replica of a bank without a roof. Jack added a few finishing touches as Harrison set up Lego mini figures.

"These are the bankers, these are the tellers, here are the security guards, and these are bystanders," Harrison explained.

"There's only one security guard at this bank," Jack stated, removing one of the police officer mini figures. He set down a blue matchbox car and picked up a novelty magic wand to use as a pointer.

"So we park the car around the corner," he narrated, pointing the magic wand at the Matchbox car, "and walk right through the front door."

"Is that your car?" Harrison wondered, knowing the details were very important, even for a fake robbery.

"Not my car," Jack responded.

"Where do we get the car?"

"I'll handle transportation," Jack said, losing patience. "All right, once we get inside—"

"What about cameras?"

Jack sighed. "Don't worry about cameras because we're not going to steal anything, remember?"

Jack moved the Han Solo mini figure and the Chewbacca mini figure into the bank. He placed Han Solo by the bank teller. "I'll get in line here—"

"Wait, I'm Han Solo," Harrison protested.

"It doesn't matter, kid."

"I'm always Han Solo. And Max is always Luke. You don't have to be Chewie. You can be Senator Palpatine. Or Jar Jar."

"There's no way I'll ever be Jar Jar," Jack scoffed. "Here, I'm Boba Fett." Jack swapped Boba Fett for Han and tossed Chewbacca aside. "Okay, so I'll create a diversion. I'll drop a juice bottle, and when the glass shatters—"

"What if they don't let you bring it in?" Harrison prodded. "The juice bottle, I mean. Sometimes there are rules, like no food or drinks."

Jack stared at Harrison a moment until he came up with a solution. "I'll just sneak it in. Okay? Stop questioning the plan."

"My dad always said plans are like skiing. You can do everything to mentally prepare for a good run, but once you get moving anything can happen. Plan for the worst, work for the best."

Jack took a few seconds to absorb such fine wisdom from a kid. Then he thought of something. "Where'd you say your parents were?"

"My mom went on vacation with her boyfriend," Harrison explained. He winced at the sound of his own voice saying "boyfriend."

"And your dad?" Jack asked.

"He died last year." Harrison dipped his head slightly. Jack's heart sank for Harrison. Jack knew what loss felt like.

"So it's just your little cousin up there watching after you and your brother?"

"Yeah," Harrison lied. He wanted to shift the conversation back to the plan. "So what's next?"

"Okay, so when the glass shatters everywhere, it'll distract the security guard, and you can slip behind the counter and into the vault." Jack moved the Han Solo Lego mini figure to the vault area. "And then I'll pretend like I'm getting paper towels from the bathroom and join you."

"Banks don't have bathrooms," Harrison countered.

"Sure they do," Jack argued.

"I've never been in a bank bathroom."

"There's definitely a bathroom. You just have to ask where it is." Jack's patience was running thin.

"I didn't build a bathroom," Harrison worried, looking down at the Lego bank.

"I'll figure it out, don't worry." Jack moved the Boba Fett Lego mini figure randomly across the bank, diverting it toward the bank vault. "Once we're both in the vault, mission accomplished. And we'll slip out as easily as we slipped in." Jack moved Han and Boba out of the vault and out the door.

Harrison stared at the Lego bank replica, not a hundred percent confident in the plan. The basement door opened and Max trotted downstairs.

"What do you want?" Harrison said, annoyed.

"Remember what Dad used to say?" Max pleaded. "If it sounds like trouble, then it probably is?"

"Wow, your dad was a fountain of advice, huh?" Jack joked.

"Go away, Max. This meeting is for bank robbers only."

"You're gonna get in trouble," Max warned.

"We're not doing anything illegal so it's fine." Harrison made a good point. He had no plans to steal money. Sneaking into a bank vault might come with some consequences, but he was only ten so it would hardly amount to a slap on the wrist.

"I have a baaaaad feeling about this." Max looked Harrison directly in the eyes. He had finally gotten Harrison's full attention. It was a line of dialogue that pretty much every main character in Star Wars said in the movies and that Harrison always recited when they played Legos together.

Harrison paused. He tried to remember the time when he and Max last played Legos. It seemed like it had been forever ago, maybe before Dad died.

"Nobody cares what you think," Harrison finally said.

"You'll be put on the Naughty List. You won't get any presents next year." Max felt sad for Harrison.

"Hello? It's Naughty Week. We're allowed to be bad," Harrison countered. "And second of all, I don't care about Christmas. I don't care about presents anymore. There's no Naughty List. It's all just a trick for parents to make their kids behave. I'd rather rob a bank."

"That's the spirit," Jack said, even though he knew first hand that there was in fact a Naughty List. He'd been on it for years.

Max turned and headed up the creaky basement stairs. Harrison lifted the Luke Skywalker Lego mini figure from the pile and stared at it in his hand.

"Are you having second thoughts?" Jack wondered. "Because...if you want to spend the last few days of Naughty Week staying up late and eating junk food and barely being naughty at all, I totally understand."

It was manipulative, but Jack made a good point. What's the fun of Naughty Week if you hold back? Harrison threw the Luke Skywalker Lego mini figure back into the pile.

"No," he stated assertively. "I'm in. I'm all in. This is gonna be awesome."

Harrison smiled wide. There was no turning back.

23

NAUGHTY WEEK: DAY 3

In the master bedroom, under a warm pile of blankets, Max and George snored soundly. Through the doorway, Harrison passed by, fully dressed and carrying a backpack. He stopped to look inside the room and peered at his brother. He wished Max was as enthusiastic about the planned fake robbery as he was. No matter, Harrison thought. He was committed with or without Max. He eyed the digital clock on Mom's bedside table. It was a little after eight a.m. Time to go.

Harrison headed down to the foyer and started pulling on his coat and hat when George arrived at the top of the stairs.

"Not so fast there, buster."

"Don't try to stop me," Harrison said, slipping on his gloves.

"I have no intention of stopping you. I just wanna settle up on a matter of a certain little deal we made before your hiney gets thrown in jail."

Harrison stared at George, unsure of what she was talking about.

"Santa's itinerary?" she reminded.

Harrison dug into his backpack. "Here," he said, handing over the wrinkled piece of paper.

"I am *so* outta here," George said, heading for the living room.

"Me too." Harrison opened the front door, and the chill of frozen morning air poured in.

"You're really gonna go through with this?" George wondered, a slight tinge of concern in her voice. "Because I'm just saying... certain naughty activities cannot be un-naughtied."

"For the last time, I'm not robbing a bank. It's just for fun. Jeez."

"Whatever you say, naughty boy." George headed for the chimney.

"You can tell Max I'll be home in a couple of hours. Nice knowing ya."

George turned and squared herself up with Harrison. "Kid, I was sent here for one reason." She waved the itinerary like a miniature flag. "Finally got what I came for. Stayed a wee bit longer than I wanted to. Had some fun, had some laughs. But if I don't get back to the ice ranch soon, the Elf-B-I are gonna start asking questions. The sooner I ditch you brats, the better."

George's comment stung Harrison, though he didn't show it. In the three days that he and Max spent with George, it felt like they had made a new friend. But like Dad used to say, all good things come to an end.

"Whatever," Harrison said. "Have a nice life."

Harrison stepped out into the cold morning, slamming the door behind him as George rolled up Santa's itinerary, stowed it in her pants, leaned forward, and shot up the chimney in a flash.

The house stood silent until the pitter-pattering of floppy-socked feet descended the stairs. Max looked into the dining room, the kitchen, and the living room. "Harrison?" he called out in a sleepy voice. "George?"

He received no answer.

24

A NOT-SO-SMART IDEA

Harrison crunched his way over the snow-packed sidewalk to the corner of the street. The industrial snowmaker and the snow machines had since disappeared, but on the roof of his house, the chimney remained damaged. The snow ramp still stood on the front lawn. Harrison wondered how long it would take for it to melt. Depending on the weather, it might be there 'til April. Mom's not going to like that much.

A lime green SmartCar pulled over to where Harrison was standing. Inside, Jack sat behind the wheel. He gave Harrison a thumbs-up, and Harrison trotted over, taking in the awkward size of the car. It was roughly the size of a golf cart. *I could drive this thing*, he thought to himself.

Harrison climbed into the seat and fastened his seatbelt. Jack reached behind the passenger's seat and grabbed some green reusable grocery bags. "Here, take these," he stated, dumping the bags in Harrison's lap.

"What am I supposed to do with these?" Harrison wondered.

"That's what you're gonna put the money in," Jack replied, matter-of-fact.

"But we're not taking any money."

"Of course," Jack explained. "We're not taking any money *out* of the bank, but it's not a fake bank robbery unless you can get the money to the doors. It's like in a video game. You find the jewels or the diamonds or whatever, then you have to get them to the end of the level. Except this time, the jewels are a couple of grocery bags full of money."

Harrison glanced suspiciously at Jack. The plan had suddenly changed since they developed it in Harrison's basement. Just yesterday, the goal was simply to get inside the bank vault. Changing the plan seemed fishy to Harrison.

Jack handed Harrison a plastic box the size of a glasses case as they drove away from the curb. Harrison opened it and looked over thin metal tools clasped in place. "What are these?"

"Locksmith tools. For the safety deposit boxes," Jack said. "Just go for two or three big ones. Use the little stick with the hook and give it a good rattle. They should come right open but don't spend too much time on it. Consider it like a bonus stage."

Harrison looked at the locksmith tools in his hand. He thought about what Max reminded him of what Dad always said. *If it looks like trouble...*

"You okay?" Jack asked. Harrison sat awfully quiet.

"You know, that actually sounds like a fun video game," Harrison piped up. "What you were saying before, about the jewels and the diamonds and the bonus level. We could probably have George develop it for us."

"George?" Jack wondered. "Little, tiny, smelly George?"

"She's good with that kind of stuff."

"Your tiny cousin George is what, like an app developer? A software engineer?"

"She's not my cousin," Harrison finally fessed up. He figured

George was halfway to the North Pole right now, so her cover story didn't matter anymore. "She's an elf."

"An elf..." Jack assumed Harrison was messing with him. "You know, people her size take offense to that."

"It's true. She's from the North Pole. She's got this little sack of Christmas dust. She can pretty much make anything. And she's a misfit elf, so I mean she'll make *anything* and doesn't worry about breaking any rules. She made us an Invisible All-Terrain Super Power Jet Mobile."

To Jack, Harrison seemed like a level-headed kid. Most kids his age stopped believing in Santa Claus, even if a small part of them knew Santa was the real deal. There was something so magical about all of it. But at some point in a kid's life, he or she crosses a natural bridge into maturity. Some teenagers and adults still wondered about the big guy in the North Pole, but not Jack. Jack knew for sure that Santa was real, for better or for worse.

"This information would have come in handy, you know, before we hatched the plan." Jack sounded disappointed.

"It doesn't matter," Harrison said. "She didn't want to get involved. She's long gone now." Harrison felt relieved that George left. It was only the third day of Naughty Week, and Harrison had had enough fun for an entire Naughty Year. Still, Harrison felt a little sad to see George go.

Jack sensed Harrison's mixed feelings. "Forget about her. The plan is rock solid. We've got nothing to worry about, right?"

Harrison shrugged.

"Look, this was your idea," Jack reminded Harrison. "You don't have to go through with it, but I'm not giving up on Naughty Week."

"I never said I was giving up on Naughty Week," Harrison responded defensively.

"Just stick to the plan, and everything'll be cool," Jack assured.

The SmartCar slowed to a stop. Jack powered down the car

and set the keys above the visor. Harrison scanned the area. They were about halfway down the block from the bank. Across the street, an RV was parked. Had Harrison known it was Jack's 1999 Bounder, his internal alarms would have told him to run away from there as fast as possible.

"Are you ready?" Jack asked, sipping from a bottle of Snapple.

Harrison set his eyes on the entrance of the bank. He was in the zone. "Let's do this."

25

THE THING ABOUT MOMS

Max sat on the living room couch with a glass bowl full of candy in his lap and the portable phone cradled against his neck. The television was muted, and Max stared idly forward as the ladies on *The View* argued about who knows what.

"Are you having a good trip?" he asked into the phone.

Seventeen hundred miles away, Mom sipped her morning coffee. Back home, she rarely could enjoy a full cup of hot coffee. Halfway through, she would inevitably be asked to toast some waffles or prepare a bowl of oatmeal. Beside her coffee mug, a book sat with a bookmark poking out three-quarters of the way through. She *never* got to read at home.

"It's been great so far," Mom said, smiling bittersweetly. Her vacation had been nice, but she felt a little homesick after a few days away. "It's been very relaxing. Dale's out on the slopes. He's a pretty good skier. Not as good as Dad was, but who is, right?"

"He was the best," Max said, remembering how fast his father could go.

"I just wanted to stay in and read," Mom admitted. "I sure miss my boys."

"We miss you too." Max turned off the TV. After so much exposure, he had become bored with television.

"I trust you're being good for Grandma?"

Max hesitated. Had Mom been in the room with him, she would absolutely see through the lie he was about to tell. "Yeah. We're being good."

"Not staying up too late? Eating too much junk food?"

Max set the bowl of candy to the side. Even candy didn't taste as sweet after eating it round the clock for seventy-two hours.

"How's your brother holding up?"

"He's doing okay," Max stated. "I don't think he likes Dale." For whatever reason, Max felt compelled to deliver that information to Mom.

"Do you like Dale?" Mom asked.

"He's really nice," Max admitted. "But he's a dentist, so he's got that going against him."

"Is Harrison there? I'd love to talk to him."

"Uh, no, he's..." Max looked around, as if that would help him come up with a great lie. "He's outside. Probably up to no good."

"Well, you keep an eye on him for me. Don't let him get into any trouble."

"'Kay," Max promised, turning the television back on.

"Be good for Grandma."

"I will." Max stared blankly at the women still arguing on *The View*. He started turning down the volume when the program was suddenly interrupted with a red "Breaking News" graphic flying across the screen. A handsome anchorman with a tan face stared forward.

"We have late breaking news this morning," the anchorman said stoically.

"Is that Grandma? Put her on," Mom said through the phone.

"No, uh, that's just the TV. Grandma's outside too," Max lied again.

"Oh, okay. Well, when she gets back, have her call me," Mom said. Max must have lingered too silently because Mom's voice shifted, as if she sensed something was up. That's the thing about moms. They always know when something is up. "Max? Is there anything you want to tell me?"

Max went to mute the volume when the news cut to a grainy black and white surveillance video of an animal shelter. All of the cages were open, and there were cats wandering around. A figure appeared in slow-motion. It was the Santa Claws Cat Burglar carrying two arms full of cats.

"If you think you've seen the Santa Claws Cat Burglar in your area," the anchorman's voice narrated as the image froze and zoomed in, "contact authorities as soon as possible. He is said to be armed—with cats—and extremely dangerous."

The footage paused on the man's face. Max's eyes widened at the sight of the image—the Santa Claws Cat Burglar was unmistakably *Jack*.

"Oh no." The words dropped out of Max's mouth compulsively. To moms, this is like a smoke alarm going off.

"What's that, hun?" Mom was now concerned.

"Nothing. Uh, okay, Mom... Gotta go. Love you!" Max hung up the phone in a panic.

On the television, Max rewound the DVR to Jack's face. In the lower portion of the screen, the text read: *Johnathan K. Dolan, a.k.a. Jack Dolan, a.k.a. The Santa Claws Cat Burglar.*

A deep, grave look of concern overcame Max's face. "Harrison..."

"I thought he looked familiar."

Max snapped his head to the sound of a woman's voice. It was George, and she was standing in the living room doorway holding Santa's itinerary and a pizza box.

"George? You're back!" Max said excitedly.

George just stared at the television screen. "I knew there was something about him, but I couldn't quite put my finger on it. I was halfway to the Pole when it hit me. That's Little Johnny Dolan, all growed up."

"Little Johnny Dolan?" Max asked, as if he should know who George was talking about.

"It's worse than I thought," George explained. She tossed the pizza box and the itinerary on a nearby loveseat and folded her arms tight across her chest. "That is one naughty dude."

26

LITTLE JOHNNY DOLAN

Schultz's Collector's Cards and Sports Memorabilia opened in Old Town Bethesda in April of 1988. Johnny Dolan was ten years old, and it had been two years since The House of Cards, his favorite baseball and football card shop in Wheaton, had closed down. Johnny visited Schultz's every week since it had opened, and he was saving his money for one single item.

Johnny loved the Baltimore Orioles. Even though they were in the middle of their worst season ever and would finish the year with 107 losses, his loyalty never waned. He collected every Oriole baseball card he could find—Eddie Murray, Mike Boddicker, and Brady Anderson were some of his favorite players. But there was one player he revered the most, one player who blew any other player out of the water, and that was Cal Ripken Jr.

Like all Orioles fans, Johnny could count on the veteran shortstop day-in and day-out. Ripken never missed a game, and he was always good for a base hit. He wasn't much of a base-stealer, but what he lacked in speed he made up in rock solid fielding abilities. In just his second full year in the Major

Leagues, Ripken led his team to victory over the Philadelphia Phillies in the 1983 World Series.

During the 1984 season, Cal Ripken Jr. solidified himself as young Johnny's favorite player when Johnny's dad took him to the home opener at Memorial Stadium. They got there early so they could catch batting practice. Johnny mustered all the courage he could to call for Cal to come over to the third base line where Johnny and his dad snuck down from their assigned upper deck seats. Johnny must have yelled loud enough because Cal trotted over, looked him square in the eye, and said, "What's your name, buddy?"

"Um, I'm Johnny Dolan," Johnny said, completely starstruck.

"Hey Johnny Dolan, I'm Cal." Johnny would never forget how blue Cal's eyes were. They were bluer than blue—blue like the Smurfs, and they shined like gemstones.

"Can I have your autograph?" Johnny asked politely.

"Sure, what can I sign?"

A crowd started to form around Johnny and his dad, wanting to get close to the All Star. Johnny worried he would miss his chance, but in the moment, he froze. Finally, his dad slipped off Johnny's brand-new Orioles baseball cap and handed it to Cal along with a permanent marker. Cal signed the orange brim of the hat and slipped it on Johnny's head.

The fans pushed forward, wanting their time with Cal, but duty called. As Cal strode off toward the infield, Johnny removed his hat to look at the signature. And there it was, written in dark black ink: *To Little Johnny Dolan. Best Wishes, Cal Ripken Jr.*

Johnny wore that same hat four years later on his way to Schultz's Collector's Cards and Sports Memorabilia, which had finally opened its doors to the public. In his pocket, Johnny had forty dollars that he had saved from mowing lawns. The money was meant for one single item: Cal Ripken Jr.'s rookie card.

Johnny knew exactly what it looked like from the August

1987 issue of Beckett Baseball Card Monthly. On the card, Ripken stood posed in his right-handed batting stance wearing his home jersey, his head tilted forward, his blue eyes peering over his left shoulder, his unseen hands gripping the bat upright behind his right shoulder, framed by the iconic 1982 Topps red-on-orange elongated vertical swoosh that bordered the left side of the trading card and turned at the bottom left corner until it ran into the name Cal Ripken. It would be the only time the position of third base ever appeared next to Ripken's name, as he transitioned to shortstop the following year.

Ripken's signature was printed in thin black lettering over the blank space of his jersey. It was back when Topps printed the player's signature on the cards. Johnny took pride that he had Cal Ripken Jr.'s real-life autograph right there on the brim of his hat. Johnny gripped the forty dollars in his hand—a combination of ones, fives, and a single ten-dollar bill that, to Johnny, smelled like fresh cut grass. As he turned down the block, he visualized the transaction for the one piece of Johnny's baseball card collection that was missing. It was to become the crown jewel.

Halfway down the block, Johnny noticed three older boys he didn't recognize coming his way. They were about fourteen, and they noticed him too. Johnny moved to the right side of the sidewalk. They shifted over, threatening to block his path. Johnny moved over to the left, and the older boys shifted too. Johnny's heartrate increased as he drew nearer. The boys were smiling now. Johnny smiled too. Maybe they were just messing with him.

Johnny slowed, and he was just ten paces away when he shifted over to the right side of the sidewalk again. The smiles on the boys' faces disappeared and, as before, they got in his way.

Johnny stopped. Maybe the boys would just walk past, he thought. But they stopped too, and stared at him like lions stalking a helpless ten-year-old boy.

Johnny started walking again, and as he neared the boys, he tried to move around them. "Excuse me," he said politely.

As he slipped to the left, trying to get around the older boys, the one wearing a Mötley Crüe T-shirt grabbed the prized Orioles hat right off his head.

"Hey!" Johnny shouted desperately. "Gimme that back!"

The boys laughed at him. Mötley Crüe held the hat high above his head as Johnny lunged for it. "Oh, you want this?" he taunted, dangling the hat out of reach.

"Come on!" Johnny jumped, flailing his arms.

Mötley Crüe looked at his friend in the Stüssy hat. Stüssy looked at the third boy who pushed his hands into his jean jacket, impressed over how much Johnny struggled for the baseball cap.

"He must really want his hat back," Jean Jacket observed.

"Oh, really," Mötley Crüe said, waving the hat out of Johnny's reach.

"What's so special about it, dork?" Stüssy teased.

Johnny suddenly turned quiet. The hat had indeed been very special to him, but the last thing he wanted was for these bullies to know why it was special.

Mötley Crüe looked at Stüssy and Jean Jacket, briefly taking his attention off Johnny. Johnny lunged once more for the hat, but Mötley Crüe pulled it up at the last second and pushed Johnny away.

"Please," Johnny begged, out of breath, "can I just have my hat back?"

And that's when Stüssy saw the black permanent marker on the brim of the hat. "Hey, whose signature is that?"

Mötley Crüe turned the hat and read the signature. "Whoa," he said, "it's signed by Cal Ripken." He read it aloud: "To Little Johnny Dolan. Best wishes."

"Awww, isn't that sweet?" Jean Jacket teased.

Johnny grabbed for it again, but Mötley Crüe turned his

shoulder, blocking the attempt as he unsnapped the clasp on the back of the hat to resize it for his own fitting. He placed it on his greasy head and turned to his friends with his hands stretched outward. "What do you guys think of my new hat?"

"Give it back!" Johnny shouted. He scanned the area for a grown-up who could come in and intervene on his behalf, but there was no one around. He thought about running up to Schultz's to find an adult, but by the time he'd get up there the teenagers would be long gone.

"You want it back," Mötley Crüe stated intimidatingly, "it's gonna cost you. How much you got?"

The image of Cal Ripken Jr.'s rookie card flashed before Johnny's eyes. He had been saving for weeks for that card. He promised the card shop's owner, Mr. Schultz, that he was going to purchase that card as soon as he had the money. There was another rookie card priced for twenty-five dollars, but it had a crease in the upper right corner. Johnny didn't want that one. He wanted the one in mint condition, so he continued saving.

But in this moment, he really wanted the hat back. He was desperate to get it back. Maybe he should just give the bullies his hard-earned forty dollars, he thought. He could save another forty dollars mowing lawns. It would only take six to eight weeks, but it could be done. There was more than one Cal Ripken Jr. rookie card but absolutely no replacement for the Orioles hat signed to Johnny by the actual Cal Ripken Jr.

"Fine," Johnny surrendered. "I have forty dollars. Take it, I don't care. Just give me my hat back."

Mötley Crüe's eyes widened, and Stüssy's jaw dropped. Forty dollars was a lot of money for three bullies to share in 1988. Jean Jacket's smile wavered awkwardly. Of the three of them, it was pretty clear that Jean Jacket seemed like he'd be the one to regret all of this one day.

"All right then," Mötley Crüe said, "fork it over." He put out his hand to collect.

"Dude," Jean Jacket interjected. "Don't take his money, just give him the hat back."

Johnny's eyes snapped to Jean Jacket. Finally, an ally. Johnny closed his fist tighter around the cash. All of this would be over soon.

"Shut up, dweeb," Mötley Crüe said to Jean Jacket. "I want his money." Mötley Crüe stretched out his hand further.

"Y'all are idiots," Jean Jacket stated, and then he started walking away. *No!* Johnny thought. The only one to come to his aid, the only one to stand up for the little guy, was now bailing. Johnny couldn't believe it. If the Founding Fathers were made up of a bunch of Jean Jackets, there would be no United States of America.

Johnny loosened his grip around the cash in his hand. He knew what had to be done to get his beloved Cal Ripken Jr.–signed Orioles hat back. It took every bit of strength for Johnny to lift his hand. He finally dropped the bills into Mötley Crüe's palm and reached for the hat. Mötley Crüe shoved the forty dollars into his pocket, then placed the hat back on his own head.

"Thanks, Little Johnny. You're so generous," he said. And then he started walking backward down the sidewalk, staring at Johnny menacingly.

"Hey, what about my hat?" Johnny pleaded.

"What hat?" Mötley Crüe said innocently as he turned around. Whether Stüssy approved of the unfair business practices that had just occurred, Johnny couldn't decipher. The bullies disappeared around the corner as Johnny stood there on the sidewalk, frozen in his misfortune.

Johnny's face turned red. A swirl of emotions cascaded through his body—disappointment, anger, rage, sadness. He whimpered as his eyes filled with tears. He wiped his eyes with his shirt, and he decided in that moment he would never allow anyone to take anything from him ever again. In fact, he was going to be the one to start taking.

And he would start right then with a certain Cal Ripken Jr. mint condition rookie card.

Johnny walked up the stairs of the Old Town Bethesda strip mall and headed into Schultz's. A few other kids and a dad stood by a glass case looking at signed baseballs. Mr. Schultz saw Johnny enter and knew exactly why he was there. Johnny had come every Saturday since the shop opened.

"There he is," he said, announcing Johnny's presence and removing the Cal Ripken Jr. rookie card from its display case. He placed it on top of the glass and moved to help the other customers.

Johnny approached the card, dejected, but also with a newfound drive to take what he felt he deserved. If he hurt someone else as much as he had been hurt, then so be it. He lifted the clear, plastic card holder that encased the baseball card and peered across the store just as Mr. Schultz ducked into the back office. Johnny seized his opportunity. In a single motion, he slipped the Cal Ripken Jr. rookie card into his right pocket and turned for the door.

Johnny never looked back. He made it down the outside stairs, through the parking lot, and to the sidewalk. Mr. Schultz must not have realized what had happened, Johnny thought, or else he'd come screaming and yelling after him. Johnny knew he could never step foot in Schultz's ever again. He turned sad at that thought, but he didn't let it shade the fact that he had a Cal Ripken Jr. mint condition rookie card in his pocket.

Johnny never got caught for what he did that day, nor did he ever confess to anyone that he took the baseball card. But come Christmas of 1988, Johnny would understand there would be severe and irreversible consequences for his actions.

27

THE BANK JOB

J ack approached the front door of the bank and pulled it open. He held it and nodded Harrison inside.

"Okay, *son*, go over there and have a seat on the couch," he stated loud enough for everyone to hear. "I'm just going to get in line and do some banking."

Harrison walked over to the waiting area with his green reusable grocery bags and plopped down on the stiff, uncomfortable bank couch. He eyed the open door to the bank vault, then looked back at Jack who was now standing behind four other bank customers. Between two teller windows, holiday-themed commercials played on a flat-screen TV.

Jack removed the Snapple bottle from his coat pocket and uncapped it for a sip. Half the juice remained in the bottle, so he tried to finish it in one big gulp, but the juice spilled down the front of his coat.

"Aw, jeez," he cried out. He tried to wipe himself with his sleeve, but he only spilled more. "For crying out loud!"

He meant to draw attention, and indeed he did. The customers turned to regard the commotion just as—on the flatscreen TV—there was breaking news about the Santa Claws Cat Burglar, and right there, on screen in high definition, appeared Jack's pixelated mug.

Jack's eyes widened at the sight of his face on television. As the customers in front of him turned back to the screen, Jack COUGH-COUGH-COUGHED for his life, anything to keep the people from looking back at the TV.

Harrison stood up from the couch, clutching his reusable grocery bags, and started wandering nonchalantly about the bank. Jack shifted his eyes from the TV, to Harrison, and to the heavy-set, hulking security guard positioned by the door.

Jack decided it was time for his special diversion. He let the Snapple bottle slip from his fingers.

CLINK, CLANK, CLUNK. The bottle bounced off the floor and rolled to Jack's feet.

"Oh gosh. Good 'ol butterfingers me. Sorry, everyone." Jack leaned down and lifted the bottle off the ground. The customers stared back at him, mostly annoyed. Jack stood upright and purposefully dropped the bottle again.

CLINK, CLANK, CLUNK. The darn thing refused to break.

"Holy carp! Saint salmon! My fingers are so dry and slippery! Good thing I kept the lid on, haha, or boy oh boy, there'd be glass everywhere. Sheesh!"

The customers turned back to the television just as Jack's image on screen transitioned to file footage of cats. Jack breathed a sigh of relief, noticing Harrison by the coffee station on the other side of the bank easing toward the gate that led to the open bank vault.

Harrison inconspicuously glanced back at Jack and nodded. Jack nodded back at Harrison. And with nobody watching except the hulking security guard, Jack lifted the Snapple bottle high into the air and slammed it down to the bank floor—CRASH!— shattering it to pieces.

"Hey!" the security guard yelled. "I saw that! Get over here."

Everyone in the bank, from the customers to the employees, was now staring at the imbecile who just broke a glass bottle on purpose. Nobody saw Harrison slip past the security gate and walk into the bank vault.

"Oh lordy, I am sooooo sorry," Jack confessed.

The security guard pointed down at the glass. "You're gonna clean that up, sir."

"You're gosh darn right," Jack said amicably. "Jeez Louise, look at that. I have done it for sure, haven't I?"

Jack headed over to the coffee station and grabbed some small, square napkins, turning just as Harrison stood at the entrance of the vault with one of his grocery bags filled with cash.

"Jack," Harrison called in an urgent, hushed tone. "Check it out—I did it!" He smiled wide. The fake bank robbery was a success. For Harrison, this is what Naughty Week was all about.

Jack couldn't believe what he was seeing. There stood a ten-year-old boy with what must have been twenty-thousand dollars in cash. Stealing a mint condition Cal Ripken Jr. rookie baseball card seemed petty in comparison.

"Holy good God," Jack said, astounded. "You really did do it."

Jack looked over his shoulder at the security guard, who was setting up a plastic yellow *Danger: Wet Surface* sign, then Jack urgently turned back to Harrison. "Well, what are you waiting for? Go fill up the other bag."

Harrison set down the grocery bag by the security gate and darted back into the vault. Jack carried over his napkins and scooped up the cash-filled grocery bag, then he walked over to the broken Snapple bottle and dropped the napkins on the puddle.

"Hey," Jack alerted the security guard. "You know there's a kid messing around in the vault?"

And just like that, Jack had sold out his partner in crime.

28

BUSTED

The security guard jumped to action, hustling to the security door, hand on his sidearm, just as Harrison exited the vault with the second grocery bag full of money.

The security guard pointed at Harrison. "You! Kid! Stop right there!"

Startled, Harrison dropped the bag and lifted his hands into the air. Stacks of one-hundred-dollar bills spilled onto the floor.

The security guard eyed the money, shocked. "You gotta be kidding me."

"Jack?" Harrison called out. For Harrison, the prank was over. Bring on the slap-on-the-wrist, he thought.

But Jack was heading for the exit. The security guard called over. "You know this kid?"

"I've never seen him in my life," Jack lied.

A grandma in her seventies next in line for the teller pointed at Jack. "That's his father," she said. "I heard him when they first came in."

On the flatscreen TV, Jack's pixelated face appeared again.

The customer in the paint-speckled coveralls behind the grandma couldn't believe it. "Oh my goodness!" he said. "It's him! It's the Santa Claws Cat Burglar!"

As Jack reached the door, Max and George burst in.

George stood in his way. "Well, well, well...if it isn't Little Johnny Dolan."

"Aw, jeez," Jack said, annoyed.

"Hey, you—where's my brother?!" Max demanded.

"Sir, stop where you are, get down on the floor, hands above your head," the security guard ordered, but Jack kept walking.

Max jumped in front of Jack. "Where's Harrison?!"

"SIR, I said don't move!" The security guard unholstered his sidearm. The customers in line gasped and panicked.

"Max!" Harrison called from the vault.

"Harrison!" Max called back.

"Nobody move!" the security guard yelled.

"Flappy, freeze!" George screamed, shoving her hands in the air.

Jack grabbed George. "I'll be taking this," he calmly stated, cradling her in his arm like a football.

"Unhand me, you lanky devil!" George demanded.

Behind the bank tellers, an alarm sounded. Jack bolted out of the bank with the grocery bag full of cash and George under his arm.

"Max! Stop him!" Harrison called from the other side of the bank. Max snapped to action, running out to follow.

The security guard grabbed Harrison's arm and handcuffed it to a handrail, then chased after Jack as sirens wailed in the distance. Harrison stood there, solemn, as he could hear the police cars draw nearer. He thought about the last fifteen minutes of his life, regretting all of it.

Tugging at his handcuffs, he understood that this was more than just a prank. He was in deep trouble.

29

THE GREAT ESCAPE

Jack rushed across the street with the sack of cash and George squirming under his grip. He hustled to where the Bounder was parked and flung open the side door. He tossed George inside and slammed the door.

"Hey! What gives, man?!" George called from inside the RV.

Max suddenly came running and jumped on Jack's back. "Let her go!"

Jack slipped the boy off his back and set him on the ground. "Shoo," he said. "Get out of here if you know what's good for you."

"Cats!" George yelled from inside. "I knew it! There's like a full litter in here!"

"I said let her go," Max repeated. He started blindly swinging closed fists at Jack's legs and stomach. "If you wanna take her, you'll have to take me too!"

"Fine," Jack said, opening the side door. "Get in."

Max pushed the hair out of his eyes and backed away. Jack took a few steps forward. "Look, kid, this just escalated, and there's no ransom without a kidnapping. You leave me no choice." Jack lunged for Max, but then George came screaming out of the Bounder, jumping on Jack's back.

"Gotcha!" she said, digging her fingernails into his shoulders.

"Jeez Louise, really?!" Jack underestimated how feisty an eight-year-old and a misfit elf could be. He pulled Max into his left arm and slipped George off his back with his right, then turned for the RV with Max and George kicking and screaming under his arms.

INSIDE THE BANK, Harrison pulled and tugged at his handcuffs. They would not budge, but he continued tugging away when the grandma in line, whose hair was so gray that it looked blue—or maybe it *was* blue—approached Harrison.

"Tsk tsk. Young man, you should be ashamed of yourself. If you were my grandson, I would be very disappointed in you."

Harrison did his best to ignore her.

"Taking people's hard-earned money like that," the grandma chastised, waving her pointer finger. "What you did was very, very naughty."

Harrison eyed her, still tugging away. He happened to agree with her, but the only thing that mattered right now was getting out of the handcuffs and helping Max and George.

"They're going to lock you up and throw away the key. I say good riddance."

Harrison furrowed his brow at the old woman, but then something occurred to him. His face lit up like he just recalled the answer to a question on a test that he studied for but somehow couldn't remember. With his free hand he dug into his pocket and retrieved the oblong case Jack handed him in the SmartCar. He unzipped it and removed a thin, pen-sized locksmith tool. Having no idea what to do, he slipped the hooked wiry part of the tool into the keyhole of the handcuffs.

"Hey. Just what do you think you're doing?" the grandma chided. "Stop that. You stop that right now, you naughty boy."

Harrison worked the lock until—SCHLICK, SCHLACK, SCHLINK—the handcuff slipped open, surprising himself *and* the grandma. Harrison shook off the tingling sensation in his wrist and darted for the exit.

"Get back here! Get back here right now, you little hoodlum!" The grandma and the rest of the customers could only watch as Harrison disappeared from the bank.

"FREEZE!" A bank security SmartCar screeched to a stop across the street from the bank, bouncing off the curb. The security guard jumped out, sidearm raised at Jack. "Put the kid and the little girl down."

"Ha ha, Max," George said amused, "that fake cop just called you a little girl. Seriously, when are you gonna get a haircut?"

"Not funny," Max struggled.

Jack spun around, ignoring the security guard. He carried Max and George to the Bounder and pushed them inside, slamming the door and locking it from the outside.

"Just what in Hades do you think you're doing?" the guard said, his sidearm still trained on Jack.

"Like it or not, these two are gonna help me do something I've been planning for a long time," Jack explained. "So if you'll excuse me."

"Stop, or I'll...or I'll..." The security guard's hands were shaking. The police sirens were getting closer, but they weren't nearly close enough to calm down the security guard.

"Or you'll what?" Jack pressed. "Or you'll throw that nice

rubber gun at me?" Jack moved around to the driver's side door and hopped in. He fired up the Bounder and pulled away as Max slammed on the metal cage that divided the cockpit from the back.

"Let us out!" he demanded.

"You should probably put on your seatbelt," Jack encouraged. "It can get a little bumpy back there."

Max finally gave up and slumped on a seat. He found the seatbelt and snapped in.

"What was that all about?" George asked.

"I was trying to rescue you."

"Well, next time you try making a dramatic rescue, maybe don't get captured." As the RV hustled down the road, a cat without any hind fur crawled onto George's lap and laid down. "Aw look at this one." George gave the mangy little creature a scratch behind the ear. "So what's your plan up there, stretch?" George wondered.

30

A NOT-SO-SMART GETAWAY

The security guard could do nothing but watch as the Bounder roared down the street. Frustrated, he threw his rubber sidearm to the ground, and it bounced off the sidewalk and popped him in the nose just as Harrison came running.

"You, get over here," the security guard said, rubbing the sting out of his nose.

The sirens got louder, the real cops only blocks away. Harrison looked at the security guard, then down the road where the Bounder disappeared around the bend, then at the lime green SmartCar he and Jack arrived in earlier.

"Son, you are in deep, deep doo-doo. Now get over here before I really lose my cool." The security guard moved toward Harrison.

Without thinking about it, Harrison sprinted to the Smart-Car. He jumped inside, found the keys where Jack left them in the visor, and started the car as the security guard hustled into the street. Harrison moved the seat forward so he could reach the pedals, then accelerated, U-turning around the security guard just as police cars screeched to a stop in front of the bank.

"You don't understand! That's my brother!" Harrison exclaimed to the security guard as he drove away.

The security guard stood in the street, yelling at the police and pointing down the road. "That way! They went that way!" He jumped into his bank security SmartCar, fastened his seatbelt, and chased after Harrison.

Harrison sped down the road, gripping the steering wheel. It was his first time driving an actual car, but it wasn't that different from operating a golf cart, which he had done the few times he played golf with Dad. The SmartCar actually handled a bit better. A few blocks down, he turned the corner onto Georgia Avenue and nearly clipped a taxi that was parked in front of an office building. Up ahead, he could see Jack's Bounder idling at a stop light.

Inside the RV, Jack ignored Max and George, who were out of their seatbelts and incessantly banging on the metal cage divider. The light turned green, and something caught his attention in his left side mirror. It was a lime green SmartCar weaving inside the lane. Jack squinted, suspecting who might be in there.

Farther back, another SmartCar rounded the corner onto Georgia Avenue. Jack had no reason to be alarmed until four police cars turned the corner, sirens blaring.

Jack floored it. Max and George fell back into their seats, and the cats yelped inside their carriers.

Harrison bypassed traffic in the bike lane and pursued closely behind the Bounder, which turned down a residential street in Harrison and Max's neighborhood. Harrison followed, inching closer.

The security SmartCar got stuck at the red light, and when it tried to navigate around traffic, it ended up blocking the four police cars, causing quite a mess of a jam.

In the neighborhood, Harrison accelerated around to the left of the RV. They were now side-by-side. "Oh God oh God oh God," Harrison murmured, doing his best to keep the vehicle from smashing into a parked car.

In the RV, Max looked out the window. "It's Harrison!"

Harrison locked eyes with Max and shouted, "Max! Hang on!" He could see that Max was trying to tell him something, but he couldn't read lips at that high speed. "What?! I can't hear—" But then he saw Max point ahead, and his lip-reading ability suddenly kicked in at forty-five miles per hour. *Look out?* Harrison wondered, his eyes trained on Max. He finally took his eyes off his brother and looked ahead.

"LOOK OUT!" Max and George shouted from inside the Bounder.

Harrison's eyes widened as he processed what he saw ahead of him: It was a monstrous rusty yellow snow plow moving a giant pile of snow from Ambler Court, and Harrison was heading straight for it. He tried to slow down, but he was traveling too fast. He wanted to turn, but there was nowhere to go.

"AAAAAAAAHHH!" He slowed the SmartCar down to about fifteen miles per hour when—PLOP—he drove into a tall pile of snow. The plow beep-beep-beeped back onto Ambler Court as the RV cruised away.

Inside the SmartCar, Harrison was frustrated and disappointed but otherwise okay. He powered down the window and climbed out, falling onto the snow. He scrambled to his feet and stepped into the middle of the road only to see the Bounder once again disappear around a corner.

As Max and George stared back toward Harrison, Jack steered the Bounder onto Colesville Road toward the Beltway. Jack moved into the turn lane and drove toward a large green highway sign that read "Washington D.C./Northern Virginia."

In the quiet neighborhood, Harrison stood there in the road, frozen in indecision as everything turned a bit darker. An eerie silence overcame the block, muted by thick clouds above. The police sirens were faint, about a mile away. Harrison looked up toward the sky as it started to snow, cold flakes landing softly on his face. If Harrison wanted to save his brother, he would need to act quick, or at least get the heck away from the car he stole and avoid being arrested. He looked down Ambler Court and saw the snow ramp in front of his house. With nowhere else to go, Harrison ran home.

31

NAUGHTY WEEK FEVER

Six and a half miles south of Silver Spring, two Georgetown University graduate students slipped out of their Dupont Circle apartment, their awareness heightened as the snow accumulated on the ground around them. The young man with overgrown hair and a gray knit Hoya hat pulled on a pair of leather gloves and scraped a handful of wet snow off the hood of a black Honda Pilot. He formed the snow into a baseball-sized snowball, took aim at a stop sign, and fired it off.

PLUFF! The snowball smashed against the stop sign, spraying snow into the frigid air. The snow started to fall heavier as day turned to dusk.

The young man's friend pulled out his iPhone and brought up his Twitter app. He scrolled through his latest tweets and found the hashtag he was seeking: #NaughtyWeek

He tapped on it, and the app redirected him to thousands of tweets. He tapped on the little square icon in the corner to compose a new tweet and began typing:

Who's up for an epic snowball fight? Dupont Circle NOW. #NaughtyWeek

Within seconds, his phone started jingling, over and over with every like and retweet. He held up the phone to show his friend in the Hoya hat. "Bro, it's blowing up," he said, stunned.

"Come on!" the young man in the Hoya hat yelled, and the grad students hustled down New Hampshire Avenue.

As they approached the circle from the northeast, they cut across the street, and snowballs rained down on them—THWAP THWAP THWAP!—followed by laughter.

They took cover behind a van and peered around the fender to get a better view. Standing on the balcony of a third-floor apartment were five college-age women in pajamas taking a break from a Netflix movie marathon.

The young women cheered and hollered. "Naughty weeeeeeeek! Whoop-whoop!" one of them shouted.

The young men quickly formed a half dozen snowballs apiece. "On my count," Hoya hat said through a wide, childlike smile. "One...two...THREE." They jumped to their feet, took aim at the balcony, and launched their snowballs—missing horribly. The neighboring residents spilled onto their balconies just as more snowballs soared their way. Groups of snowball-wielding neighbors and friends appeared from all directions.

Taking snowball fire from all sides, Hoya hat and his buddy dashed for cover just as the college-age women from the third floor flooded out of the building, in hats, boots, and winter coats pulled over their pajamas. They screeched with delight as they joined sides with the grad students and pushed forward against an oncoming onslaught of snowballs.

Within minutes, hundreds of people—from teenagers to retirees—descended on Dupont Circle for what would become the most epic snowball fight in Washington, D.C.'s history.

32

NAUGHTY WEEK CONSEQUENCES

Harrison entered his house and headed straight into the living room. He sat on the couch, near tears, and scanned the walls and shelves. All around him were framed family photographs—his mom, his dad, Max, and himself. He felt something digging into his leg. It was a half-eaten Butterfinger bar. He took a bite, but it no longer tasted sweet.

Unsure of what to do next, Harrison turned on the television. The local news was mid-report: "Naughty Week fever spreads!" the anchor announced. As he spoke, footage of the epic snowball fight appeared on screen. Hundreds of people throwing snowballs and having the times of their lives.

"More than five hundred have gathered at Dupont Circle for what appears to be a spontaneous snowball fight," the anchor continued. "The informal gathering, reportedly organized via Twitter using the hashtag 'Naughty Week,' has resulted in some very minor injuries and a few broken windows, as is to be expected, I suppose. Authorities were called to the scene but quickly joined in the fun." The video on screen cut to Washington, D.C. police officers throwing snowballs at Washington, D.C. firefighters.

Click. Harrison turned off the TV. The house was solemnly quiet. "I messed up everything," he confessed to no one in particular.

Suddenly, the phone rang. Harrison looked at the portable receiver. He didn't want to answer. What if it was Mom? He was finished lying to her, but how could he possibly tell her the truth? What could he possibly say? *Hi Mom, how's your trip? By the way, Max and an elf from the North Pole were kidnapped by the Santa Claws Cat Burglar and you may never see your youngest son again.*

He resigned himself to his fate and answered.

"Hello?"

On the other end, there was only silence.

"Hello? Who's there?"

Finally, a voice: "Hello, Harrison. How are you?" It sounded like Max, but something was off. In fact, it actually sounded like Max was doing an impersonation of a robot.

"Max?"

"Yes," Max confirmed. It was definitely Max.

"Max!" Harrison shouted, sitting up. "Are you okay?"

"Yes, we are ock," the voice explained. Harrison squinted. *Ock?* That sounded weird.

"I mean, we are...oh-kay."

"Max?"

"Unfortunately, George and I have been kidnapped by a very nice man who has not hurt us at all and are being held for dansom...I mean ransom."

Something finally dawned on Harrison. "All right, ha ha, I get it. This is some special Max voice app, right?"

On the other end of the line, silence.

"Jack, this isn't funny," Harrison said. "I thought we were

friends. And George, I'm actually quite disappointed in you for helping him with a Max voice app."

Still no answer from the other side of the line.

"Put Max on!" Harrison demanded.

Inside Jack's Bounder, Jack sat in the driver's seat, trying to tap words into an app on his cell phone. "Your stupid app is totally glitchy," he said to George.

"As if it's user-ready. It hasn't even been beta tested yet. Jeez," George said defensively from the other side of the metal cage separator. "Anyway, in my experience, it's usually the user, never the app. Don't blame the app for being a moron."

"Just take it," Jack said, unlocking the cage. He handed Max the phone.

"Harrison, it's me," Max said.

"No, it sounds exactly the same," Harrison responded.

"I swear, it's me," Max argued. He didn't much like being accused of sounding like a robot.

"Prove it," Harrison demanded.

"What? How?"

"I don't know," Harrison said. "Tell me something only you and me know."

"Like what?"

Harrison thought a moment, his eyes scanning the room. His gaze landed on a photo of Max, Harrison, and Dad on a ski trip. "Okay... What was the last thing Dad said to us? Before he...died."

The phone line went silent. Harrison shifted on the couch, losing patience. "Whatever," he dismissed. "Nice joke. I'm hanging up now." But he didn't move. On the other end, he could hear a sniffling sound. Harrison knew that sound. He heard it dozens of times at bedtime during the months after their father passed away.

In the RV, Max wiped tears off his face and sniffled again. "He told us..." Another sniffle as tears poured from his eyes. "He said...'Be good for your mom.'"

And then Max lost it, crying uncontrollably. In the living room, Harrison's eyes filled with tears. They had one rule to live by, their dad's golden rule, and they broke it.

"Max," Harrison started. "Don't worry about anything. I'm gonna find you and get you home. I promise."

"But Harrison," Max stated through sobs. "Jack says he won't let us go until he gets the money."

Jack suddenly grabbed the phone from Max. "Fifty thousand dollars. I already asked the elf and she claims she can't just make it. I'm serious. Get the money by tomorrow or I'm gonna take your brother to Canada and make him go to school year-round. I'm not fooling around, kid. And no cops. I don't have to remind you that *you* just robbed a bank, do I? You're facing thirty years to life, buddy."

Click. The line went dead. Harrison's eyes widened as the consequences of his actions sunk in.

"Oh no," he said to nobody. "What have I done? I have to get them back... But I don't have fifty thousand dollars. Nobody has fifty thousand dollars. What do I do?"

He started pacing around the living room, thinking, weighing his options. He couldn't call Mom. Not yet at least. She would be so mad, and that's not productive. He couldn't go to the police for obvious reasons. He was a wanted man now. He thought about the next thirty years of his life and what that might be like if he spent those years in jail.

He knew he had to help Max, but he couldn't do it alone. Who could possibly help him? Mrs. Klopek across the street? She'd just turn him over to the police.

He paced and paced and searched his mind for ideas. His eyes wandered about the room, seeking a solution. Finally, he saw George's pizza box on the loveseat. And right beside the pizza box, a rolled up piece of paper. Harrison picked it up and unrolled it—it was Santa Claus's travel itinerary.

"*Santa,*" Harrison said to himself. If there was anyone out there who could help, few were better qualified than Santa Claus. Harrison read over the itinerary, zeroing in on the destination. *Boca Raton, Florida.* His heart sunk. Florida was about a hundred thousand miles away. How could he possibly get to Santa? It's not like he could just hop on an airplane. Maybe there was a bus that went that far south, but how long would that take? A week? Harrison didn't have that much time. And he couldn't just pick up the phone and call.

Harrison stared out the window to the backyard, utterly stumped. And that's when he realized the solution was hiding in plain sight, staring him directly in the face.

33

DAD

"If you believe in something strongly enough," Dad said to Harrison from his hospital bed, "then you can make it happen."

Harrison gazed at his father. His face appeared pale and chalky, his lips were dry and chapped, his hair stringy and thin. He had not shaved in a few days, and whiskers grew sharp out of his chin.

"It's going to take hard work. It's going to take a lot of hard work." Dad turned his head toward Harrison and made eye contact. "Do you hear me, Harrison?"

Harrison nodded.

"If you have a dream, and you don't take action to pursue your dream, then that's all it will ever be. A dream." Dad reached for a plastic cup of ice water beside the bed. It took all of his strength, but eventually he grasped it and brought the straw to his mouth. He drank in small sips.

"But if you believe in something strongly enough," Dad repeated for emphasis, "then you *will* make it happen."

Harrison nodded again, even though he no longer shared that

point of view. For the last year, Harrison believed his father would get better. He believed in the doctors and the medicine so strongly that there was no question in his mind that Dad couldn't beat the illness. There was not much Harrison could do for his father in terms of taking action, but he did not stop believing.

"The doctors are saying I may not be around much longer," Dad said. "That's their opinion." The corner of Dad's dry mouth curled up into a smile. "Never lose faith, son. Never stop believing."

Harrison held in his tears as best he could. He didn't want to cry in front of his father. Earlier, a nurse came to the waiting room and told Harrison that his father wanted to see him, just him. Dad had called Harrison in for a man-to-man talk, so he braced himself for the worst. Harrison was only nine, but he committed himself to taking the news like a man. Sitting there by his dying father, however, it would prove to be a more challenging endeavor than he expected.

"You're going to get better," Harrison said, choking up.

"I still believe, buddy," Dad said with a smile. A tear dripped from his left eye, and it surprised Harrison that even dads cry sometimes. Harrison wiped his own eyes.

"I love you, Dad." Harrison lost it. He leaned forward and hugged his dad.

"I love you too, buddy."

34

THE SANTA SOLUTION

Harrison ran upstairs to his closet and dug out a sweatshirt, his winter coat, a knit hat, gloves, a scarf, and a pair of goggles. He would need everything he could find to keep himself warm for the trip he was about to embark on. He slipped ski pants over his sweatpants and pulled a pair of boots over warm, wool socks.

He ran downstairs and out the back door. He approached a blue tarp that covered something and ripped it down, revealing absolutely nothing. He stepped forward and reached his hand out, as if to flip a switch. Suddenly, it appeared before him. The one and only Invisible All-Terrain Super Power Jet Mobile.

Harrison climbed on, strapped a helmet over his knit hat, and pressed the ignition button. The Jet Mobile's engine purred, and the navigation screen blinked to life. Harrison typed in the destination: The Boca Raton Inn. Boca Raton, Florida.

As police sirens entered the neighborhood, the Invisible All-Terrain Super Power Jet Mobile lifted high into the air. Once Harrison floated well above the trees, he stuck out his finger and pressed the invisibility button and—FWOOP—he disappeared.

35

PRISONERS IN AN RV

Somewhere deep inside an underground parking garage, Max and George sat on opposite sides of a crate playing cards as cats roamed freely about the RV. They had only driven forty-five minutes from Silver Spring, and Jack refused to tell them where they were before he locked the side door from the outside and left to run an errand. Max had taken enough field trips in school to know that by the looks of it, they were somewhere in Washington, D.C.

"Do you have any eights?" George asked.

"Go fish," Max responded.

George took a card from the top of the deck and quickly glanced at it. "Darn it, I never get my wish."

"This is stupid," Max complained.

"It's Go Fish, what do you expect?" George replied. "Wanna switch to Gin Rummy or Spit?" A cell phone chimed. George looked through the cage separator at her phone, which was set beside her little sack of Christmas dust. "Man, I bet that snowball fight was epic. My Twitter won't shut up."

"We should be trying to escape," Max stated. He slammed

down his cards on the crate and walked over to the Bounder's side door. He pulled at the handle. He kicked. He punched. But the door wouldn't budge.

"There you go, flappy," George said sarcastically. "Maybe it'll open this time." George quickly sneaked a peak at Max's cards just as Max turned around.

"Hey!"

"What? They were literally falling off the crate," George lied. "You should thank me. Seriously, they would have spilled all over, and then I'd be able to see what you had."

"You're not just a misfit elf. You're a cheat and a liar," Max accused.

George set down her cards and pressed her hand to her chest, pretending to be offended. "Whoa. I mean...whoa. Now that just hurts."

Max grabbed the crate and slammed it against the RV's side door. The playing cards fluttered everywhere.

"Hey! We're playing cards here!" George protested.

Once again, the door would not budge. Exhausted and out of breath, Max plopped down in his seat. He looked at George. "So what did you do?"

"What did I do what?" George said, annoyed.

"Why are you a misfit elf?"

"Beats me, flappy." George spun in her seat, turning away from Max.

"You've gotta have some idea," Max pressed. "When I get in trouble and lose privileges, there's usually a reason. Mom doesn't punish me for nothing."

"I am an adult elf," George explained. "I don't get punished or grounded or sent to my room. I get sanctioned. There's a huge difference."

"So why were you...sanctioned?" Max's interest had been elevated.

George took a moment, lost in thought before offering Max a dismissive shrug. "It's stupid."

Max just stared at George, politely waiting for an explanation. It's what Mom would do to him when she wanted him to talk, like the time Max got in trouble at school for throwing mud at the fifth-grade windows. Mom simply asked him why he would do such a thing and turned quiet. Max shrugged—much like George had done a second ago—and then after a minute of painful silence, Max opened up to his mother, explaining that all the other boys were throwing mud and he didn't want to be made fun of for being a good boy and not joining in with the cool kids.

Finally, George spoke up. "You really wanna hear this?"

Max nodded, still not wanting to break his silence, allowing George the opportunity to open up.

"So I'm on the toyline, right?" George started. "Plastics. Most toys are plastic these days, so most of us elves work in plastics. All of the old farts are still carving wood, but trust me—wood will be out by the time you have kids. It's not sustainable, and there's this ongoing ethical debate—deforestation and all that. Anyway, now that everything's plastic, I believe—and this is just me speaking— I believe the work is getting sloppy. And now that there are so many kids in the world, The Big Man had to come up with this special solution, this powder." George pointed a thumb over her shoulder to the little sack next to her phone. "Christmas dust. And that was like back in the early 90s, and since then craftsmanship has completely gone out the window. So what do I do? I ask for a transfer to electronics. Every year, I put in a request—and this has been going on since the first iPod hit the market. So I ask for a transfer and year after year Old Santy Pants refuses. And this year he tells me he's actually getting rid of the entire electronics department because Christmas dust does the work of like a hundred elves, so he's gonna take all the elves from electronics and throw 'em into plastics and I'm like, come on, enough's enough. I got friends in electronics that'll retire before they go back to plastics. I mean, am I right?"

Max stared at George quietly a moment before finally blinking. "Yeah."

"Thank you! So what do I do?" George leaned forward for emphasis. "I get rid of the Christmas dust."

Max's eyes widened, deeply enthralled by George's story. "You stole the Christmas dust?!"

"I hid it," George confessed. "Talk about madness up at the Pole, right? It was like *whoa*—beautiful chaos."

"So there weren't enough toys this year?" Max wondered.

George's demeanor shifted, knowing what she did was wrong. "Almost," she admitted. "Eventually, Dr. Jelly Belly cried loud enough, and then Mrs. Claus got involved—and believe me, you do *not* want to cross that woman. So in order to avoid an international crisis, I caved and returned the Christmas dust. Boy, was Santa mad."

"So that's why you're a misfit elf," Max said, putting the pieces together.

"I gave it back!" George argued. "Christmas went off without a hitch! So why am I being punished?"

"Well, you can't always do what you want because you don't agree with something. You still have to follow the rules." Max's explanation seemed incredibly rational.

"I thought you were on my side, Mr. Naughty Week-ling."

Max didn't like being called names, but he knew George felt bad about what she did. "I am on your side," Max explained. "We're a team, you and me. We should have each other's backs. If I was in the North Pole when you hid the Christmas dust, then I probably would have recommended you give it back because it sounds like there are a lot of people counting on it. I wouldn't want to get you in trouble, but think of the trouble you'd be in— and the trouble Santa would be in—if you *didn't* give it back."

George nodded somberly yet gratefully.

"But now that I think of it," Max mused, "if you believe against something strongly enough, then you need to *change* the rules. Like Martin Luther King did."

George raised her eyebrows at Max's deep and sudden wisdom.

"My dad taught me that," he admitted. "Still, it doesn't sound like Christmas dust is the problem. It sounds like the problem is you're not happy in your job."

"Exactly." She appreciated what a good friend Max had become to her over the last few days.

"Is there anything more you can do to get transferred to electronics? I mean, besides filling out paperwork every year?"

George thought about it. "I suppose I could set a meeting and present my case."

"Maybe meet with Mrs. Claus first. It sounds like she's got a lot of say in what goes on up there. Maybe if you make your case to her, she can give a recommendation to Santa."

It was a brilliant idea, and it made perfect sense as soon as George heard it. "That's a pretty darn good idea. Thanks, flappy," she said appreciatively, opening up her arms. "Bring it in."

Max moved in for a hug, and they squeezed each other tight like old friends. As they separated, Max got serious. "Now let's get out of here instead of sitting on our butts. Jack could be back any minute."

"It's pointless, kid. Let's just wait it out."

Max didn't want to give up that easily. And then something occurred to him. "The Christmas dust! That's it!" he said excitedly. "Can't you use your Christmas dust to make something that'll help us escape?"

"Sure, flappy, anything you want. Just reach through the cage and get it."

Max peered through the metal cage separator and eyed the

little sack of Christmas dust on the dashboard beside George's phone.

"Or," George continued, "we could wait for the right opportunity. Jack doesn't have the slightest idea what it does. So we wait it out, and then when the time is right, we grab it."

"Or," Max countered, "we could find something to use as a tool, slip it through the cage thing, and get it right now." He started searching the RV for some sort of tool—something long enough and thin enough to fit through the ping-pong ball–sized holes of the metal cage separator. "Come on, help!"

George leaned forward in her seat. "Wait! I have a better idea." Her tone was enthusiastically sarcastic. "We can strap these cats to our backs, okay, and pretend we're cats, see, and when Jack robs his next house and leaves a cat, we'll be free!"

"Very funny," Max said, and then continued his search. He moved to the back of the Bounder and dug through a makeshift closet. He pushed hanging shirts aside, and a size medium flannel button-down slipped off its hanger. Max looked up at the swinging wire hanger. "I've got it! We can use this!" He grabbed the wire hanger and started untwisting the hook as George looked on, sincerely impressed.

36

VIRGINIA TO FLORIDA IN UNDER
AN HOUR

Snow began to fall over Greensboro, North Carolina. Up until a half an hour ago, it had been an otherwise clear night. The Piedmont Winterfest rang in full blast downtown, the outdoor skating rink filled to capacity and more excited skaters waiting in line.

For anyone listening closely, he or she might have heard the exhilarating scream of a ten-year-old boy soaring high above in his Invisible All-Terrain Super Power Jet Mobile.

WHOOOOSH! Harrison flew overhead, gone as quickly as he arrived. Below, a seven-year-old girl strapping on ice skates looked up, thinking she heard something. But by the time she had scanned the cold night's sky, Harrison was long gone.

WHOOOOOOOOOOSH! Harrison soared through the sky— over clouds, under clouds—wind whipping over his face. He navigated the Jet Mobile up and over ridges, down between a clearing in the trees, over rooftops, and under bridges.

A smile froze on Harrison's face, for he knew what it must be like for Santa if Santa was riding an Invisible All-Terrain Super Power Jet Mobile.

37

DINNER IN VAIL

Thousands of miles away, Mom and Dale sat down to a quiet, candlelit dinner. Dale looked across the table. He could tell something weighed heavily on Mom's mind.

"Is the wine okay?" he asked gently.

Mom smiled. "It's fine."

"The fish?"

Mom picked at her dinner. "It's delicious. Thank you, Dale."

"A penny for your thoughts," Dale suggested.

Mom smiled again at his turn of phrase. Not many people talked like Dale. "A penny for your thoughts" was something Dale *would* say. "I was just thinking about New Year's Eve. I've never missed New Year's Eve with my boys. Since they were young, we'd stay up 'til midnight and right at twelve o'clock we'd go outside and bang pots and pans until someone—usually Mrs. Klopek—yelled at us to stop. This one year when they were younger, Harrison ran across the freezing sidewalk barefoot like he was crossing hot coals, all while Max sang 'Happy Birthday'— the only song he knew. It was...fun." She grinned at the memory.

Dale leaned forward and pressed his hand on top of Mom's.

"I'll call the airline. We'll head back tomorrow."

"No, no, no," Mom argued. "You made these big plans for New Year's. Just the two of us. I know how much you're looking forward to it. I don't want to ruin anything."

"Are you sure?" Dale prodded.

"I'm sure. Trust me, I'm sure," Mom said, unsure. "I'm just gonna try the house again, make sure everyone's all right."

Mom stood up from the dinner table and scooped her phone from the kitchen counter. She tapped "Home" on the top of her favorites and listened impatiently as it rang and rang until the voicemail message came on: "You have reached the Fulwell residence," Harrison said in a goofy voice, "We can't come to the phone right now..."

Mom hanged up and tapped the next name on her favorites list, "Grandma." The line rang and rang. Giving up, Mom disconnected the call and sighed. "Maybe my mom took them to a movie or something," she said, reassuring herself as she sat back down to finish her meal.

Dale could tell she deeply missed her boys. It had only been three days, but for a mom who spent the last year of her life keeping her boys as close as she could after the passing of her husband, seventy-two hours felt like an eternity.

Dale reached for his phone and searched for a number. "I'm calling the airline. We'll head back tomorrow."

Mom smiled appreciatively. The vacation had been exactly what she needed—some much-needed time to herself—but she was ready to return home. "See if there's something in the afternoon," she suggested. "We can do a little skiing in the morning. We shouldn't let all this fresh snow go to waste."

Dale nodded as he dialed the airline. Mom took a cleansing breath, feeling much better about everything. Little did she know that thousands of miles to the east, her boys were far from home, separated by hundreds of miles.

38

MAKING CAT BURGLAR HISTORY

On the dashboard of the Bounder, George's little sack of Christmas dust rested beside her cell phone, two adult arms' lengths from the metal cage separator that divided Max and George from their freedom. The little maroon pouch was bound by a thin ribbon tied with a neat little loop, and by the looks of it, it weighed about a pound.

Max and George gripped a crudely straightened wire hanger, which they pushed through one of the holes in the metal cage.

"Easy... Easy... Easy does it," George coached.

"Almost...careful George," Max worried.

The hook of the wire hanger approached the sack. Max and George rotated the wire to get it into position.

"Okay, gentle now. Hook the loop," George guided.

"I'm trying, I'm trying."

The hook grazed the loop and nearly caught the ribbon. The wire bumped the sack of Christmas dust, and it began to slide down the dash toward the windshield.

"No no no! Stop!" Max shouted. His heart pounded heavier in his chest.

"What did you do?!" George accused, her anxiety level heightened.

"I didn't do anything!"

"You did *something*."

"We have to hurry," Max urged. "I don't know how much time we have."

∿

INDEED, Max and George were running out of time, as Jack had stepped off a train at the Foggy Bottom Metro Station and started for the escalators. He carried a plastic shopping bag of supplies.

As he stepped onto the escalator and rose to the ground level, Jack whistled "Silver Bells," his favorite Christmas carol. While most people considered the tune rather generic, opting for Mariah Carey or one of those novelty songs like "Grandma Got Run Over by a Reindeer," Jack enjoyed the melodic croon of Bing Crosby's "Silver Bells." It reminded him of sitting in front of the fireplace as a child, watching football with his dad and eating sandwiches on some lazy Sunday in December while his mother decorated the house.

At the snowy surface, Jack headed down to I Street and turned the corner toward a parking structure. His whistling echoed off the surrounding buildings and high into the air. It was a quiet night. The whistling carried all the way up to the roof of an apartment building, where a newly engaged young man and woman toasted champagne and blissfully sang along with the stranger down below. From their vantage point, they could see down to where I Street merged with Pennsylvania Avenue, and even farther east toward the most identifiable mansion in Washington, D.C.

∿

In the RV, Max and George inched the wire hook closer and closer. It wobbled as it hovered over the sack of Christmas dust. They lowered it to the ribbon loop and—hooked it!

Max and George gasped with relief, but they still had work to do. They carefully rotated the straightened hanger and let the loop slip down the wire, securing it onto the hook. They pulled the hook back and the Christmas dust lifted safely off the dashboard.

"Careful there, flappy."

The sack inched closer and closer toward them. George slipped her fingers through the cage, ready to receive when, from outside the Bounder, the sound of footsteps, keys, the door unlocking, and—*Jack*.

"What the hay?" Jack blurted, confused, watching the little sack of dust float through the air in the front cab of the RV. He grabbed the dangling sack mid-air and tossed his plastic bag of supplies onto the passenger's seat.

Jack stared at Max and George, holding the sack of Christmas dust up to his face. "I take it this is important?"

NO CHILDREN, PLEASE

A t the Boca Raton Inn, the night guard sat in the glass-enclosed security hut reading yesterday's sports section when—WHOOOOSH—something flew past at lightning speed.

The guard set down his newspaper and leaned out the window. He looked left, and he looked right. He pulled his body back into the guard hut and scanned the security monitors. Nothing seemed out of the ordinary, so he sat back down and continued reading.

At the far edge of the parking lot, just outside the reach of security cameras, Harrison parked the Jet Mobile between two palm trees. He stepped off and engaged the cloaking device, and —THWAP—the Jet Mobile disappeared.

Harrison took in his surroundings. The parking lot was only half full. A soft, warm breeze blew through the palm trees above. Stars shined overhead in the night's sky. Harrison started toward the resort, sneaking from one palm tree to another. As he approached the entrance, he heard the sound of feet shuffling and ducked under a sign.

A group of retirees passed, flip-flopping their way home from a night walk. Lying flat on the ground, Harrison peered up from his hiding spot and read the sign: *The Boca Raton Inn. 21+ (No Children, Please)*. Harrison realized that finding Santa at a grown-ups–only resort might be more difficult than he anticipated.

He thought of all the lies he could tell if he were caught. It was Naughty Week, after all, so lies were part of the game. Maybe he could say he was just visiting his grandma. Maybe he could say he was lost. Or maybe he should just forget about Naughty Week and tell the truth. Nobody ever got in extra trouble for telling the truth. Getting caught in a lie? That was a different story.

As Harrison thought of all the different lies and telling the truth and the various consequences he might face, his exhausted eyes closed, and he drifted to sleep.

40

THE PNL

I n the driver's seat of the Bounder, Jack held the little sack of Christmas dust in his hand while Max and George sat quietly on the other side of the cage separator.

"So this is some kind of magic dust, right?" he wondered. "The little pizza eater brought this from the North Pole? Is that it?"

"I don't know what you're talking about." Max leaned forward to drive his point home. "She's my cousin."

"That's not what your brother told me," Jack said confidently. "That's right, Harrison already spilled the beans. Too trusting, that one. He'll never make it as a legit thief."

"My brother is not a thief! You *made* him steal that money!"

"Yeah, sure, explain that to the cops." Jack's shoulders sunk ever so slightly, as if he knew exactly how futile an endeavor it was to try to lie to the police when they already knew the truth.

"So now what?" George chimed in. "What's your next move, Little Johnny?"

Jack shot George a look of disdain. She had clearly said something to bother him.

"We gonna rob a house or what? There's like half a dozen cats back here. Does that mean six more houses?" George reached out and scratched behind a cat's ears. The cat climbed onto her lap.

"Joke all you want, but I take this very seriously," Jack stated. "I am passionate about my vocation as a cat burglar."

George scratched the cat's neck with both hands. "But don't you think you're taking this whole thing a bit too literally? I mean, I don't think it's actually a rule that when you become a cat burglar you're required to use actual cats. It sounds like you just made that up, or you didn't actually know because you're actually not all that bad."

Jack ignored her. "You see, I'm a man of opportunity. And when opportunity comes a-knocking, better not answer because it might just be me stealing from you. For there isn't a house I can't burgle."

"Burglarize," Max corrected.

"And I'm gonna prove that tomorrow," Jack continued, "because tomorrow, in honor of the New Year, we're gonna rob the most impenetrable house on the planet."

"Brangelina's house?" George wondered.

"Iron Man's house?" Max guessed.

"No, dummies, we're gonna rob the White House." It sounded utterly ridiculous, but Jack was utterly serious.

"That is the most preposterous thing I have ever heard, and I work with people named Peppercorn and Cootie," George commented.

"Jack," Max said with a warning tone, "you're gonna regret what you're doing once Naughty Week is over."

"No, I don't think so," Jack replied. "Naughty Week is a year-round enterprise for me."

"It doesn't have to be." Max always saw the good in people. With Jack, he could tell that deep down there was a nice, responsible person in there. After all, he made everyone wear seatbelts during their escape from the bank.

Jack eyed the rearview mirror, finding Max in the back. "Oh yes it does, kid. Once I broke bad, I couldn't ever go back."

"So it's true," George stated. "Little Johnny is on Santa's PNL."

"I swear on my mother's grave, if you call me Little Johnny one more time, I will chop you up and feed you to the cats."

"Your mom's dead?" Max asked empathetically.

"No, it was just a figure of speech."

George gave Jack a knowing side-eye glance. "Chop us up and feed us to the cats? Oh, come on. You're not the violent kind. You're just...misunderstood. Am I right?"

"Quiet back there," Jack demanded.

George folded her arms across her chest, sizing up Jack. It was as if she had long ago read one of Santa's confidential files on the guy and had now suddenly recalled every snippet of information. She leaned over to Max. "Still has some unresolved issues."

"I said quiet!" Jack's face turned tomato-red.

"What happened?" Max whispered to George.

George banged on the metal cage separator. "Yo, stretch. Do you want to tell him...or should I?"

"Tell him what? There's nothing to tell, so be quiet and go to sleep. Lights out, time for sleep." Jack pulled his coat over his shoulder and closed his eyes.

"Tell me what?"

"Well, Max...it's like this. You see, Jack—our kidnapper there —was the youngest kid ever, and I mean in the history of Christmas, to be placed on Santa's PNL."

"PNL?"

George squared off, looking Max dead in the eye. *The Permanent Naughty List.*

"Entirely not my fault and totally unfair," Jack complained from the front seat.

"Listen to me, Max," George continued. "There's only about two dozen people on the Permanent Naughty List."

"Permanent Naughty List, what a joke." Jack forced a laughed.

"You'd think there'd be more, but it takes a very naughty person to be placed on the PNL."

"So I'm on the Permanent Naughty List. So what. Big deal. Who cares." Jack pretended to go to sleep again.

"Now I don't know exactly what happened," George mused, "but I've heard the rumors."

"You don't know anything," Jack said under his winter coat.

George looked into Max's eyes, her face overcome with sorrow. "The thing about the Permanent Naughty List...once you're on it, that's it. You could be a saint for the rest of your life, a real study in piety, but it don't matter one bit. Nothing matters. Once you're on the list, game over. Santa has *never* taken anyone off the Permanent Naughty List. Ever."

"Wow, I guess that's why they call it 'permanent,'" Jack said sarcastically.

Max absorded the dour information. He looked toward the front seat. "Wow, Jack. That totally stinks."

The RV turned eerily quiet as Jack reflected on his life, and the one decision that changed everything. Finally, he pulled the coat off his head. "It was one time. And I had my reasons. Santa probably wanted to make an example out of me. For the record, the punishment absolutely did not fit the crime."

"I don't know exactly what he did," George said, "but you've gotta do something really bad to be put on Santa's PNL. I mean really bad."

Max could hardly imagine what Jack did. He needed to know, if nothing more than to know what kinds of behavior to avoid. "What did you do?"

Jack turned and looked at Max. He remembered being Max's age. He remembered how simple life was, and then how complicated things got after one misguided decision. He believed Santa Claus did, in fact, make an example of him, so that kids around the world would know that stealing was one of the worst crimes a child could commit. He wanted to explain to Max what happened, he wanted to warn him. But he was too embarrassed.

"Storytime is over," Jack said, pulling his coat back over his shoulder. "Get some sleep. Big day tomorrow. Robbing the White House. It's never been done before. Making cat burglar history. Good night. Sleep tight."

At the mention of the White House, something occurred to George. "Jack? Robbing the White House sounds cool and all, but how exactly do you plan on getting past security?"

George didn't expect an answer, but she also didn't expect Jack to be snoring like a baby that quickly. She gave Max a reassuring wink. "Get some sleep, kid. We're gonna need it."

41

NAUGHTY WEEK: DAY 4

A smooth pair of bare feet with red and green painted toenails stepped lightly across the cool pavement of the sidewalk before coming to a sudden halt. They turned onto the dewy grass and walked toward the signpost where Harrison slept.

One of the feet nudged Harrison gently. Harrison stirred, then opened his eyes. Looking up, he saw a white-haired, soft-skinned, kind-looking older woman backlit by Florida's rising sun. She could have been in her fifties, or she could have been 110. She smiled youthfully and warmly, but it was also a smile of concern.

"Young man, children aren't allowed to be at this resort."

Harrison nodded and sat up, rubbing the sleep out of his eyes and the dew off his cheek.

"Goodness, did you sleep here all night?" she continued. "Your mother must be worried sick."

Harrison fought back tears. He thought about his mom and how disappointed she would have been in his behavior.

"Come along. We'll sort this out." The woman started for the entrance to the resort, but Harrison didn't budge. She stopped and turned around, folding her arms across her chest. "It's all right, dear."

Harrison still didn't move. Technically, she was a stranger, and Harrison hadn't had the greatest experience with strangers this week.

The woman stood patiently. Finally, she reached out her hand to let him know everything was going to be just fine. "Come now, Harrison."

Now she had Harrison's full attention. He looked at her unblinking. How the heck did she know his name? Harrison tried to reason—maybe this was one of Grandma's friends, maybe she was a preschool teacher he couldn't remember, maybe he was talking in his sleep and happened to introduce himself. None of that would have been accurate, however. For there would be no reason for Harrison to know that the woman addressing him was Mrs. Claus.

42

THE SKI LIFT

Mom and Dale spent their last morning in Vail on the slopes. Dale booked them an early afternoon flight, and they wanted to take advantage of the freshly fallen powder. Mom had a sincerely wonderful week with Dale, but she was eager to get home. Halfway up the ski lift, her cell phone rang. She pulled off her right glove and dug for her phone.

"It's Mrs. Klopek," she stated before answering. "Hello, Mrs. Klopek, I'm surprised to hear from you. How's everything going back in the neighborhood?" She looked at Dale as she listened to Mrs. Klopek on the other end. "Wait, what? I don't understand. What about a snow machine?"

Mom's cell phone beeped, another call coming in. She looked at her phone screen. "That's my mother on the other line," she said to Mrs. Klopek, "hang on a sec." She tapped the answer button and switched calls. "Mom? How's everything going with the kids?"

She listened intently, her face growing concerned. "My kids," she emphasized. "Your grandchildren? You're with Harrison and Max, right?"

As she listened, Dale could tell something was very wrong. Mom looked at Dale, shocked, confused, and worried. "My mother's flying back from Hawaii. She's been on a cruise all week. Harrison and Max have been alone this whole time!"

She dangled there with Dale, creeping slowly up the ski lift. There may have been no worse place for a mother to receive such news.

"Let's go back and pack," Dale insisted. "We'll get to the airport as soon as possible."

"I am a terrible mother."

"No, that's not true. Now, what exactly happened?"

Mom wiped away a tear. "How could I leave my kids unsupervised? I deserve to go to jail."

"Don't blame yourself. She was there. Your mother was there. We both saw her. I confirmed with her."

"And then she left?"

"I told her the week of New Year's. She confirmed."

"The week *of* New Year's? Isn't that the week *after* New Year's?"

"No, it's the week of New Year's. Before New Year's."

Mom looked at Dale, utterly confused.

"Obviously, she got the dates mixed up. Obviously, it's a huge misunderstanding." Dale felt terrible. If it was anyone's fault, it was probably definitely his. He assured Mom he took care of all of the childcare arrangements. But whatever the case, the dates had been mixed up, and this was, in fact, a huge, once-in-a-lifetime misunderstanding.

"Misunderstanding, right. I'm sure Child Protective Services gets that one a lot."

The conversations Dale had with Grandma during the weeks leading up to Christmas played over and over in his head. He thought he told her they would be leaving the day after Christmas—*the week of New Year's*. Somehow, maybe, Grandma registered him saying their travel dates started the day after New

Year's. And then something occurred to Dale. "Wait. You spoke to your mother on the phone the night we arrived here. Was that not her?"

Mom considered the phone call she had with Grandma earlier in the week. "Now that I think about it, something was a little off about that conversation. I couldn't put my finger on it at the time."

"Do you think your boys faked the phone call?"

"That's crazy. Like they hired someone to pretend to be Grandma?" Mom thought about it a little more. Her boys were pretty darned resourceful. "Oh my God, I'm an idiot," she said, covering her face with her hands, the severity of the situation weighing heavily. "I should have never gone on vacation. There is no vacation when you're a mom. This was a stupid idea."

Dale looked at her, a little hurt by the statement but otherwise calm. "Our flight leaves in three hours. You'll be home by dinnertime." He placed a comforting hand on her shoulder.

"Oh, Dale," Mom said, tears flowing down her face. She was disappointed in herself, yes, but she also desperately missed her boys.

Dale pulled her close to comfort her. "Everything is going to be okay. I love you, Jenny."

She wrapped her arms around Dale. "I love you too."

They reached the top of the ski lift and raced down the slope. It was time to go home.

43

SANTA ALWAYS KNOWS

Harrison sat quietly on a soft, velvety couch in one of the Boca Raton Inn's master suites. He scanned the room and regarded how nicely maintained the suite had been kept nearly a week into someone's vacation. When his family went on vacation, there would be junk everywhere. Mostly it was Harrison's and Max's junk, but lots of it nonetheless.

Mrs. Claus carried in a tray of hot cocoa and crumpets and placed it on a small table in front of Harrison. "Santa will be in the spa all morning. I should tell you he does not want to be disturbed. It's been a rough year for him." She sat in a chair that matched the couch and held a mug of hot cocoa with both hands.

Harrison sipped from his mug. The rich chocolate coated his mouth like no powder-packet mixture could ever dream to. For whatever reason it made him think of the creamy chocolate river from Roald Dahl's *Charlie and the Chocolate Factory*, which was one of the books he fondly remembers reading before bed with Dad.

"It was left to Santa by a family in Germany, the hot cocoa.

Good, isn't it?" Harrison nodded appreciatively. "So," Mrs. Claus continued, "are you going to tell me why you're here?"

Harrison inhaled deeply and exhaled slowly. "Mrs. Claus, I did some bad things. I just wanted to have some fun. I mean, you know, because it's Naughty Week. I didn't think anyone would get hurt. Or that I'd cause so much trouble."

Mrs. Claus set down her hot cocoa, disappointed. "Dear boy, I should not have to tell you there is no such thing as Naughty Week."

Harrison blinked at Mrs. Claus, legitimately surprised. "There's not? How could that be?"

"Naughty Week is a myth that's been passed down for decades."

"Decades?"

"Ever since Santa and I decided to go on vacation the week after Christmas, rumors about seven full days of mischief spread like frosting on a warm cake. I don't care where you heard about it or who might have planted that idea in your head. The fact remains that Santa knows. Santa *always* knows."

"That's what my mom says," Harrison confessed.

"You need to listen to your mother more."

Harrison took a moment, then looked at Mrs. Claus guiltily. "He *always* knows?"

"There is an entire Naughty/Nice Department at the North Pole. They report to Santa every Thursday, even when Santa's on vacation." She lifted her mug of hot cocoa and took a conservative yet satisfying sip. Mrs. Claus loved hot cocoa.

Harrison's eyes turned worried. "Oh, man, this is terrible. I've ruined everything. And now my brother's in trouble. George too."

"George?" Mrs. Claus asked. Like Santa, she knew all the children of the world and their siblings. There was no George in Harrison's family.

"She's one of Santa's elves," Harrison explained.

Mrs. Claus's perpetually comforting gaze suddenly disappeared as she realized something dire. *"George."* She touched her fingertips to her lips with urgency. "Oh, dear. This is more serious than I thought."

"I'm really worried about my brother," Harrison admitted.

Mrs. Claus stood and hastily cleaned up. She removed the mug of cocoa from Harrison's hand, set the dirty dishes on the tray, and carried them to the kitchenette. "Of course you are, dear. But if your brother is with George, then I have a feeling he will be okay. George is...well, she is a very *willful* elf."

Mrs. Claus slipped on a pair of flip-flops and headed for the door. "Let's go, shall we?"

"Go where?"

"Where do you think?"

Harrison stared into Mrs. Claus's stern yet sympathetic eyes as it dawned on him that he was about to interrupt the coveted morning spa treatments of the one and only BMOC.

44

GROUP D

Looking every part the tourists, Jack, Max, and George stood in a long line of people outside the White House waiting for their tour group to be called. Jack carried a duffel bag over his shoulder.

As Max stared ahead at the home of the President of the United States, he wondered about the nature of what they were doing. "It doesn't have to be like this," he said, trying to reason with Jack. "I'm sure if you asked really nicely and promised to be good for the rest of your life, Santa will take you off the Permanent Naughty List. Wouldn't that be better than stealing a few keepsakes from President Obama?"

Jack pretended like he didn't hear Max. He stared straight ahead, going over the plan.

"Hmm, not likely there, flappy," George explained. "It's never happened before in history. *In history.*"

Jack finally looked down at Max and George. "It doesn't matter. I stopped caring long ago."

"Yeah, I can tell," Max observed as he looked over the long line of tourists. "You know, I can just scream for help."

"Not if you ever want to see your mother and brother again," Jack smiled. "I hear the year-round schools in Canada don't let out until four p.m."

Max wanted to call Jack's bluff, but Jack was also just crazy enough to follow through with such a threat. He had nothing to lose. "I don't get it. What do you think you're gonna do when you get in there?" Max made a good point. The White House was probably the most secure house in the world.

Jack pulled the sack of Christmas dust out of his pocket and spun it around on his finger through the ribbon. "Wait and see, kiddo. Wait and see."

George eyed the Christmas dust. "That's a very unstable formula, mister. Please don't swing it around like that."

She jumped for the sack, but Jack quickly lifted it out of her reach. He squeezed the Christmas dust in his hand. "Look, you two, if things go according to plan, you'll be free in an hour."

Max looked ahead at the tourist's entrance. "I gotta admit, it's pretty cool that we get to see the White House." Max thought of one of the many times his mom and dad took Harrison and him to Washington, D.C. to go sightseeing. When they got to the White House, the line extended all the way to Pennsylvania Avenue, so they decided to go to the National Air and Space Museum instead. They had been to the Air and Space Museum about a trillion times. Max always wondered what it would be like to visit the White House. "Do we get to meet President Obama?"

"I met the president once," George declared. "Well, before he was famous. By accident, actually. Hawaii, right before Y2K. It's kind of a funny story."

Jack squeezed the bridge of his nose with his thumb and forefinger. "Would you two please be quiet? I'm trying to get mentally prepared here." From the duffel bag over his shoulder came a muted *meow*.

George pointed at the duffel bag. "Is the cat mentally preparing itself, too?"

"Quiet."

"Come on, seriously, is the poor creature necessary?" George argued. "What if it doesn't get along with the president's dog? What-its-face, Bo? What if Bo and little Whiskers here can't coexist in peace? We could have a situation on our hands."

"Shut up, shut up."

Max stood up tall. "You're crazy if you think I'm gonna stand around while you rob the president's house. *My* president's house."

"Yeah, that's our boy in there!" George cupped her hands and yelled toward the White House. "I got yo back, prez!"

They were starting to draw attention from the tourists around them in line. Lucky for Jack, neither group appeared to speak English. Jack smiled at each group as if to suggest everything was okay before leaning down to Max's and George's eye level. "Oh, you're both so patriotic. I hope you're this patriotic when you're taking Canadian history in your new school in your new country."

"He's bluffing," George challenged.

"You're bluffing," Max taunted.

"You want to cry for the Secret Service and find out? Or do you want a nice tour of the White House and then go home to your mommy?" Jack flashed the Christmas dust again.

Max turned silent at the mere mention of his mother. He missed her and wanted to see her as soon as she got home from Vail. Little did he know she was on an airplane at that very moment.

"Bluff-ing," George sang.

"And you," Jack poked a finger at George's chest, "Little Miss Misfit Elf. You think Santa will believe you had nothing to do with this? The Elf-Bureau-of-Investigation or whatever is gonna find Christmas dust residue all over the place. You'll be banished from the North Pole. A total outcast. Consider yourself lucky to end up in Canada."

George went quiet, but only for a moment as something dawned on her. "How do you know about the Elf B.I.?"

Before Jack could answer, the tour leader arrived. "Group D? May I please have Group D line up for the tour?"

"That's us," Jack said, pushing Max and George along. "Move it."

Max took in the grandness of the White House as the herd of tourists moved toward the entrance.

45

THE RELAXATION ROOM

Harrison walked through the halls of the Boca Raton Inn, trailing a few paces behind Mrs. Claus who flip-flopped her way toward the second-floor spa. Harrison knew they were getting closer because it smelled stronger and stronger of flowers.

Mrs. Claus stopped at the front entrance of the spa. As Harrison caught up, he noticed a sign on the frosted glass that read "By Appointment Only." Mrs. Claus opened the door. "In you go. He should be in the Relaxation Room."

"Aren't you coming?" Harrison wondered. Her presence felt calm and reassuring.

Mrs. Claus looked Harrison directly in the eye. "No, dear. This is something you must do alone."

Harrison took a deep breath and crossed into the spa's waiting room where a female attendant in a white short-sleeve polo shirt and white pants looked up from a computer screen. "Relaxation Room?" Harrison asked. The attendant squinted at him curiously, then pointed the pink eraser of her pencil to another door, as if she knew with whom this boy had an appointment.

The Relaxation Room was a round, sparsely decorated room filled with flowers, soft light, and plush furniture. Atmospheric music played peacefully through hidden speakers. Harrison entered and found a large-framed, white-haired man in a terry cloth robe sitting with his back toward the entrance. He was reading an iPad and sipping cucumber iced water.

As Harrison circled around, he didn't take his eyes off the white-haired man. Once he came into the man's field of view, the man looked up from his iPad and planted his impossibly crystal blue eyes directly on Harrison. Harrison froze.

"Well...hello there," Santa Claus greeted.

Tears formed in Harrison's eyes. Harrison had never felt so much regret for his actions in his entire life, and now it was time to face the consequences.

Santa set down his iPad and motioned to a plush white chair on the other side of a coffee table. "Please. Have a seat and tell ole Santa what's troubling you."

46

CODE ORANGE IN THE MAP ROOM

A s Group D moved through the White House Map Room, Jack lagged behind with Max and George. Jack scanned the room for any sort of valuables he might want to take, but he sensed a presence behind him and nonchalantly moved for the exit.

"Keep it moving, folks," the Secret Service officer warned. He wore sunglasses and probably never smiled.

Jack shuffled Max and George through the door. "Let's go, kids. Stop dragging your feet."

"We're not dragging our feet, you're dragging your feet," George complained, pushing Jack's hands away.

"Shut your face and walk," Jack whispered.

The secret service man removed his sunglasses. "Is there a problem here?"

"No problem," Jack assured.

"Then move it along." The secret service man placed his sunglasses back on.

"No problem...an invisibility blanket can't solve!" Jack

whipped out the Christmas dust and spiked a pinch to the floor. But nothing happened.

The Secret Service man started toward Jack. "Sir, I'm going to have to escort you and your little girls off the premises."

"I'm not a kid!" George complained.

"I'm not a girl!" Max shouted, flipping his hair out of his eyes.

"Come with me please." The Secret Service man was not fooling around.

"How come it didn't work?" Jack was baffled. The one thing his entire plan hinged on did not come to fruition. This was a major problem.

George looked at Jack incredulously. "Because you're not an elf. Duh. And why is 'invisibility' so popular this year? Invisible this, invisible that. It's like this year's Tickle Me Elmo."

"I'm not going to ask again," the Secret Service man stated. "Follow me, or you'll all be placed under arrest."

Jack pressed the Christmas dust into George's hands. "Quick, do an invisibility blanket."

"Sorry, I left my wand back at Hogwarts," George quipped.

"Do it."

"No."

"Yes."

"Make me."

"Fine." Jack grabbed George's hand, dipped it into the Christmas dust, and flung it onto the floor and—POOF!—a strangely translucent blanket materialized. "Ha!" Jack yelped with delight.

The Secret Service man charged Jack, but Jack threw the invisibility blanket over himself, Max, and George. They disappeared, and the Secret Service man stopped dead in his tracks, unsure of what just happened. He lifted his wrist microphone up to his lips. "Mama Bird, this is Eagle Six. We have a Code Orange in the Map Room. I repeat, we have Code Orange in the Map Room. Requesting lockdown immediately."

He could hear footsteps shuffling in the direction of the Diplomatic Room and ran toward them when out of thin air, Jack's foot appeared, tripping the Secret Service man and sending him to the floor. Jack chuckled as his foot disappeared again, and the three of them shuffled out the door.

47

A CONFESSION TO SANTA

Harrison sat perched in a chair with his gaze turned down. He could not look Santa in the eyes. He knew if he did, he would probably cry again, and he hated that he cried in front of Jolly Old Saint Nick.

"I've been...really naughty," Harrison confessed. "I mean, like, really horribly naughty."

Santa sighed, leaning back in his chair. He scratched his chin through his beard as he listened.

Harrison finally looked up and met Santa in the eyes. "I mean, *really* bad."

"Okay, I get it. You've been naughty."

"I fake-robbed a bank, but then it turned into an actual robbery," Harrison unloaded, "and then I became connected to a kidnapping, and now I'm an accessory to the Santa Claws Cat Burglar and I'm wanted in all fifty states."

"Wow, all fifty states, huh? That *is* naughty."

"I need your help," Harrison pleaded. "No one else can help me."

Santa touched the tips of his fingers together calmly. "I come across this every year in one form or another. 'Naughty Week' is it?" Harrison sunk in his chair, guilty as charged. "You thought because I was on vacation, you had license to do whatever you wanted without consequence."

"I'm so sorry, Santa."

Santa stroked his beard. He was bothered. "What I don't get, what really irks me—regardless of whether Naughty Week is real or not—is that most people would choose to be good." The Big Man leaned forward and placed his elbows on his knees. "Why should I help you? When you so consciously chose to be naughty?"

Harrison didn't have an answer. He thought about Max. He thought about Dad. He thought that maybe all of this was about him and Max strangely honoring his father's memory in some way. But then he thought that if Dad spent Naughty Week with them, there was no way Harrison would have robbed a bank. *If it looks like trouble*, would have been his advice. Why didn't Harrison heed his father's advice during the one week he was supposed to be honoring his memory?

Santa lifted his iPad and scrolled through an app. "What would your mother think? Why, I'd imagine she'd be pretty disappointed." Harrison slouched even deeper, as if he couldn't possibly feel worse.

"And to have to come home early from her vacation and clean up this mess," Santa continued. Harrison looked up, surprised. "That's right. She's on her way right now." He tapped the screen of his iPad. "Santa knows, son. Santa always knows."

Harrison inhaled deeply, trying to keep it together. "I just wish she didn't go on vacation. And I wish she wasn't dating stupid Dale, and I wish Dad was still alive so everything could go back to normal. I just want everything to go back to the way it was." Tears flowed down his cheeks.

Santa nodded warmly. "Son, there are things Santa just

doesn't have the power to fix. I truly wish this weren't the case. Your letters last year, well, they broke my heart. And then you stopped writing, you stopped believing in the magic of Christmas, and that saddened me even more. But believe me, Harrison, if I could bring back your dad, I absolutely would."

"Why can't it just be me and my mom and Max? Why can't Dale just go away?"

"Dale," Santa repeated. "I know this Dale. He's a good man, an honest man. Always gets positive reviews from the Naughty/Nice Department. One of the many few grown-ups who still writes me letters, but he never asks for a thing for himself. I visit him anyway because of those letters. He leaves me dental floss instead of cookies." Santa chuckled to himself, and Harrison noticed his belly jiggled ever so slightly.

"You know, Dale understood your mom was missing her family," Santa explained. "He went out of his way to change their flight so she could come home early and be with you and Max."

"Dale did that?"

"I think what you may be having trouble with, Harrison, is learning to accept things out of your control. Trying to change your mother's feelings about Dale may only make matters worse. Sometimes you need to accept things for what they are. Hang onto the good memories you've made, cherish those, but then be open to making new ones in the future. Does that make sense?"

Harrison nodded. Everything Santa said, he sort of already knew to be true. Acceptance was the greatest hurdle.

Santa tapped his iPad. "Now there's still the matter of Max and George."

Harrison sat up straight and looked Santa Claus in the eye, prepared to sacrifice everything to make a deal. "Santa, I promise I will never ask for another present for the rest of my life if you can help me find Max. He's my best friend, and I don't know what I'd do if anything happens to him. Please! Please help me, Santa.

If there's a black list or something for super naughty kids like me, then write my name in permanent marker, I don't care. I just want to be home with my brother."

Santa stared deeply into Harrison's soul. He could tell this ten-year-old boy was fully contrite. Santa got up from his chair. He stood a lot taller than Harrison imagined as he took a cleansing sip of his cucumber water and switched off his iPad. "Well then. Let's go."

48

@DAREALGEORGEELF

Back in the Claus' master suite, Santa hovered over a laptop with Harrison beside him. Santa had changed into a cozy pair of corduroy pants and a red flannel. For a big guy, Santa Claus could move pretty fast.

Santa loaded a web page. "Every elf has a tracking app on his or her cell phone in case of emergency." On the laptop screen appeared a customized version of Google Earth. Beacons flashed on different parts of the globe—from the North Pole to the tropics.

Santa scanned the screen and isolated different sections. "Showing clusters in Hawaii, Fiji, the Bahamas, Cayman Islands." He could feel Harrison looking at him. "I'm not the only one who takes a vacation this week."

Santa power-typed, and the Google Earth image zoomed into the United States' Eastern Seaboard. A few clusters of beacons blinked in New York City and Southern Florida. "Hmm," he stroked his beard, "since George is alone, there should at least be one beacon in the Washington, D.C. area."

Santa zoomed in farther. On the laptop screen, nothing

blinked over Washington, D.C., Virginia, Maryland, or West Virginia. "Peculiar," Santa wondered.

"Jack said he'd take them to Canada if he didn't get the money he was asking for," Harrison worried.

"We should still be able to see the beacon," Santa said, perplexed. And then he suddenly realized something. "*George.* She must have disabled her tracking app. And she wonders why she's a misfit elf."

"She did circulate that memo on privacy." Mrs. Claus arrived, bringing in two cups of warm milk. "Anyway, I told you not to rely on a basic tracking app. What if they lose their phones? What if they're on a cruise and drop it in the ocean?"

"It's for their own safety," Santa replied, sipping his mug of milk appreciatively.

Harrison stared at the computer screen. "What are we gonna do? How are we gonna find them?"

Santa stroked his beard again. "I'm not entirely sure." Harrison looked at Santa. Was he really going to give up that easily?

Mrs. Claus leaned over her husband and typed something into the web browser. "There are probably dozens of ways to find her," she said as she loaded Twitter.

"My elves are forbidden to be on social media," Santa dismissed.

"Call it a hunch." Mrs. Claus typed something into the search bar. The page loaded, and the top Twitter search result showed a user named @DaRealGeorgeElf with a little blue verified check mark next to the handle. "How about that. TheRealGeorgeElf is checking in at...the White House."

Harrison squinted at the screen. "They're at the White House?"

"We can't be sure of anything," Santa argued.

Suddenly the Twitter page auto-loaded, and a new tweet

appeared: "OMG the Linkn bedrm is DOPE!!!!!" It received dozens of likes and retweets within seconds.

Santa stared at the tweet. "I have no idea what that means. Is that some sort of code language?"

"It means they're still at the White House!" Harrison said excitedly. He was relieved to know that George and Max were likely safe and sound. He turned to Santa with an idea. "We can take the Super Power Jet Mobile. It's in the parking lot."

"No," Santa replied, "We'll need something faster."

"I've already called for them," Mrs. Claus stated.

Minutes later, Santa, Harrison, and Mrs. Claus marched through the rooftop door. Santa whistled sharply, and a team of eight muscly reindeer glided to a landing.

Harrison's eyes nearly fell out of his skull. "Wow, they seem so much bigger in person."

Santa helped Harrison into the sleigh. Mrs. Claus handed Santa his off-season coat and wrapped Harrison in a blanket. "It'll be cold up there, but it shouldn't take long. Stay warm, dear."

Harrison smiled at Mrs. Claus appreciatively. "Thank you, Mrs. Claus. For everything." He then turned to Santa. "Are you sure this will go faster than my All-Terrain Super Power Jet Mobile?"

Santa eyed Harrison, a tad insulted. "Buckle up, kid." He then squared his shoulders and tugged on the reigns. "ON DASHER, ON DANCER, ON PRANCER AND VIXEN..."

As the reindeer soared into the air, Mrs. Claus waved goodbye from the roof.

49

THE LINCOLN BEDROOM

Jack filled his duffel bag with trinkets and treasures from the White House's most famous guest room, nonchalantly whistling "Walking in a Winter Wonderland." George lay on the bed tooling around on her cell phone as Max sat bored in a Woodrow Wilson–era chair. A cat meowed from somewhere under the bed.

"Do you guys have the fart app? It's genius," George chuckled to herself. She tapped her screen —FLPTHSP, FLSHPT, FLTHPT.

Jack moved across the room, grabbing anything he thought might have value. "Please be quiet for five more minutes. I promise, it'll all be over then."

Max rested his head on his fist. "That's what you said in the Roosevelt Room."

"Are you saying I'm getting greedy?" Jack placed a pewter framed photo of John F. Kennedy in his bag. "Okay, maybe I am." He thought better of it and returned the photo to the bedside table.

"How do you know this stuff's even worth anything?" Max wondered.

"It doesn't really matter. People pay top dollar for White House junk."

"People pay top dollar for White House junk," echoed a voice that sounded remarkably like President Obama. George held up her phone and smiled wide. "Just whipped up this bad boy— Yadda Yadda Obama—president voice app. I mean, brilliant, right?"

Max spun into an upside-down position with his arms folded and stared out the pair of French doors of the Lincoln Bedroom. Outside, snow cascaded onto the White House lawn.

"One more room, then we're done. I swear. I still have space in my bag." Jack zipped up the duffel bag.

Max moaned as the cat climbed onto the chair.

"Give me two minutes, then we're gone." Jack pulled the duffel bag over his shoulder. "I wanna get my hands on some jewelry."

George didn't budge. "I'm not snooping through the First Family's bedroom. Some things can't be unseen."

Suddenly, George's phone dinged an alert. She quickly sat up straight. "Whoa," she uttered.

"What's your problem?" Jack said, annoyed.

"It's not me with the problem, bub. It's you."

"Oh yeah, why's that?"

George looked Jack directly in the eyes, as serious as a coal-filled stocking. "He's coming."

50

"WITH MARSHMALLOWS"

Santa's reindeer rocketed into Washington, D.C. airspace, descending through the clouds, and soaring past the Washington Monument. They circled the White House and landed smoothly on the roof. As Harrison and Santa climbed out of the sleigh, a half dozen Secret Service men and women swarmed and surrounded them, guns drawn.

"Freeze!" a Secret Service woman shouted. "Hands against the sleigh."

Santa placed his hands against the sleigh, and Harrison did the same. "Nice work, Janice," Santa called over his shoulder. "My authorization is in my left coat pocket."

Janice reached into his coat pocket and removed a passport-like document as Santa looked down at Harrison. "I'm the only person in the world who has clearance to land an aircraft on the White House." He nodded toward Janice. "And it's their job to make sure I'm really me."

Janice read the clearance document, then placed it back in Santa's pocket. "Hot cocoa?" she asked curiously.

"With *marshmallows*," Santa responded, winking at Harrison. It was some kind of secondary clearance code.

"Good to see you back so soon, Mr. Claus," Janice smiled at Santa. She gestured to the rest of the Secret Service to stand down. "What is the purpose of your visit?"

"We have reason to believe the Santa Claws Cat Burglar is in the White House right now." Santa's directness matched Janice's.

"The Lincoln Bedroom, to be exact," Harrison chimed in. "He kidnapped my brother and one of Santa's elves."

"Not possible," Janice assured. "They couldn't have gotten past security."

Santa placed a hand on Janice's shoulder. "You underestimate my elf, Janice."

Trusting the graveness of Santa's tone, Janice nodded and started for the rooftop access door. "Come with me."

51

ESCAPE FROM THE WHITE HOUSE

Max heard a commotion coming from the hall. He flipped right-side-up in his chair and headed for the door to have a look.

"What is it? What's going on?" Jack asked, concealing his concern.

Max peeked through an opened crack at the door. "Uh, Jack? I think they know you're here."

Jack darted to the door to have a look for himself. Through the thin gap in the door, he could see Secret Service men and women racing up and down the hallway and speaking into the wrist microphones. "Scanning East Wing bedrooms, still no sign of intruders," one of them said.

"Intruders?" Max whispered.

"Congratulations, kiddo, you're a cat burglar now." Jack closed the door and quietly turned the lock.

"I am not," Max argued.

"Are so."

"Am not!" Max tempered the volume of his voice.

"It's over, Little Johnny. Time to hang up your cat burglar cleats," George stated as the cat meowed on the bed.

Jack looked at George and got an idea. "You. Make me some kind of escape vehicle. I'm going out the window."

"Jeez, seriously?" George sat up on the bed. "First of all, you'll have to be more specific. Is specificity too much to ask these days? Second of all, *no*."

"Don't make me force your hand again," Jack warned.

"You know what? Whatever. If it gets you out of my face, then fine." George held out her hand for the sack of Christmas dust.

"No. What are you doing?" Max worried. "Don't help him, he'll get away."

"So he gets away. Doesn't affect me in the slightest. It's a cold, dark world, flappy." George hopped off the bed. "Stand back, stretch," she said as she prepared a pinch of Christmas dust.

Jack pulled Max safely back as George snapped the Christmas dust to the floor and—POOF—an Invisible All-Terrain Super Power Jet Mobile appeared.

Jack's eyes widened. "My word. Does it fly?"

"Like the wind, baby," George said. "I wish I could tell you she was one of a kind, but that'd be a big fat lie."

Jack pushed open one of the French doors, climbed on the Jet Mobile, and fired it up. "Nice knowing ya, kid," he said to Max and—WHOOOOOOSH—he was gone.

Max turned to George accusingly. "I can't believe you helped him escape!"

George shrugged. "What difference does it make? Any minute now, Santa's gonna walk through that door. And when he sees me here, he'll sanction me again for another year. You get to go home to your family. Me? Nobody cares about me in the Pole."

WHOOOOOOOOSH—Jack returned as quickly as he departed. He grabbed Max and pulled him onto the Jet Mobile.

"Hey!" Max kicked and screamed.

"Yo! What are you doing, man?!" George demanded.

"A little insurance couldn't hurt," Jack stated.

George quickly jumped in front of the Jet Mobile. "That wasn't the deal. You can't take the boy."

"I'm changing the deal."

Max screamed and punched uncontrollably. George screamed at Jack. Jack screamed at George. The cat hissed on the bed.

In the hallway, Santa, Harrison, and Janice heard the screams. "Max!" Harrison shouted, running toward the sound.

Inside the Lincoln Bedroom, Jack pushed George aside. With one leg pinning down Max, he edged the Jet Mobile toward the French doors when, suddenly, the door burst open.

"Harrison!" Max shouted.

"Max!" Harrison yelled.

"Jeez Louise," Jack complained.

Harrison sprinted across the room and jumped on Jack's back as Max slapped at Jack's face. Overwhelmed, Jack shook them both off and shuffled to the open French doors and— WHOOOOOSH—he was gone.

Harrison and Max hugged each other tightly, brothers safely reunited, as Santa and Janice entered the room.

Janice hustled to the open French doors and lifted her wrist mic to her mouth. "Two intruders in custody, one escaped out the window heading north. Notify Metro D.C. Police and Maryland State Troopers."

Santa Claus approached George, disappointed. "George. I am glad to see you are safe. But you helped that man get away? I just don't understand. And you wonder why you're sanctioned?"

"I only did it for flappy over there," George explained. "If I didn't make the stupid Super Power Jet thing, who knows what would have happened in here once the Secret Service showed up. I didn't want Max to get hurt."

Max smiled, overhearing this.

"And don't worry about Little Johnny Dolan. I outfitted his Super Power Jet Mobile with a tracking chip and whipped up this app." George launched the app and showed Santa her phone. On its screen, a beacon flashed, indicating Jack's location. George tossed the phone to Janice. "There's your guy."

Santa looked at George proudly and a little surprised at what George was capable of. "I told you not to underestimate my elf, Janice."

"So am I in deep trouble?" George wondered. "I probably deserve to be banished from the North Pole."

Santa appeared surprised at her statement. "Don't ever say that. You are family, George. And you always will be."

George looked up at Santa and smiled. "Aw, c'mere, you big lug," she said as she pulled Santa into a hug.

Janice touched her ear, listening to the Secret Service chatter. "They got the vehicle."

"Wow, that was fast." Harrison couldn't believe it.

"No sign of Dolan. He must have ditched," Janice reported as she returned the iPhone to George.

George had no contingency plan for Jack abandoning the Super Power Jet Mobile. She looked at Santa. "What? I tried."

"At least we've ID'd him," Janice confirmed. "It shouldn't be long before he's in custody. Now if you don't mind, for security measures I need to escort you back to your transport."

"Transport?" Max wondered. He looked at Harrison, who smiled knowingly at his younger brother.

From the door, a man's voice called inside. "Is everything under control in here?"

Harrison, Max, George, and Santa turned toward the voice. Janice immediately stood at attention. "Yes, sir. A few holiday decorations appear to be missing, but nothing of significant value," she reported.

And just like that, in walked President Barack Obama—The Big Chief, Mr. Prezzy-Prez-Prez, #44, The BMOUSA. The room turned reverently silent.

"Good," Barack said as he nodded to Santa and smiled. "Santa."

"Barry," Santa greeted him kindly.

"Who's responsible for all of this?" Barack said.

"Not me," said a voice that sounded just like the President's. "I voted for the other guy." Everyone looked at George who was sheepishly holding her phone. "Pretty cool, right, Santa? I made it. You just type in the words, and the app does the rest."

Santa turned to Barack. "Pay her no mind, sir. That's George. She's one of my more...imaginative elves."

"Is that an app with my voice?" asked Barack. "That *is* pretty cool." George smiled proudly as Barack looked around the room. "Now is someone going to tell me what's going on?"

Harrison stepped forward, ready to own up to the leader of the free world. "It's all my fault, sir. I'm responsible."

Barack took a breath and nodded. "Come with me," he stated, then turned out of the Lincoln Bedroom.

YOU MAY NOW TURN ON YOUR CELLULAR DEVICES

M om and Dale waited impatiently in their seats as the airplane taxied to the gate at Dulles Airport. Mom pressed her phone to her ear, listening to voicemail.

"Five messages from my mother," she relayed. "She's beside herself. But it's not her fault. I should be put in jail for what I've done."

Dale took her hand in his as he squinted out the window, beckoning the airport terminal closer. "Don't beat yourself up. Let's just deboard, grab our bags as quickly as possible, and get you home."

"Another message, not sure who this is," Mom said curiously. She listened, squeezing Dale's hand. "She's saying the boys are fine."

"Well, that's a relief," Dale offered.

Mom looked at the number on her phone screen. "Florida area code." She listened again. "Do we know a 'Mrs. Claus'?"

A CONFESSION TO PRESIDENT BARACK OBAMA

The Vermeil Room, a grand sitting room on the ground level of the White House, is located just below the Lincoln Bedroom. Harrison sat on an antique sofa with red paisley upholstering. Santa and President Obama flanked him in armchairs.

As Harrison scanned the room, he couldn't help but notice the art on the walls—all portraits of women. Behind him hung an elegant portrait of Jacqueline Kennedy, whom he knew to be the wife of John F. Kennedy. He recognized some of the other last names on plaques, and it occurred to him that all of the subjects in the paintings must have been First Ladies. He wondered when Mrs. Obama would have her portrait up, and where it would go as the walls were already pretty crowded.

Harrison's eyes met the president's, who sat in his chair cross-legged with his hands in his lap. He seemed pretty patient, for a president. "I'm sorry to ruin your holidays," Harrison admitted.

"I'm sorry Santa had to cut short his vacation," President Obama stated. "*He's* the hardest working man on the planet." The president leaned forward and placed his elbows on his knees. "So what's this all about?"

"What is it ever about?" Santa stated. "The decisions we make on a daily basis guide our paths in life. Some are guided by a moral compass, some are led by self-interest. Some choose compassion. Some choose apathy. Some simply refuse to help anybody but themselves. Or their good deeds are done for selfish reasons. And this clears a path for an individual to become entirely self-absorbed, which in my mind goes against the very foundation of Christmas. So, given who I am and my role in all of this, I need to account for that." He looked disappointedly at Harrison.

Harrison's head sunk. "I get it. I was selfish and I screwed everything up. I don't deserve presents for what I did. Maybe not ever. I guess I just really wanted Naughty Week to be real."

"Oh, so this is a Naughty Week thing," Barack stated. "I hate to break it to you, but Santa? This guy *always* knows when you've been good or bad."

"Yeah, that's pretty clear to me now."

Santa eyed Harrison. "It's unfortunate. But in a case like this, I have no choice but to add another name to the Permanent Naughty List."

Harrison's nodded. "I understand, Santa."

"So...*permanent*?" Barack questioned. "Once someone is on the list, he or she can never be taken off? The decision is final?"

Santa nodded. "Little Johnny Dolan—the Santa Claws Cat Burglar who just escaped out the Lincoln Bedroom window— he's been on the list since he was ten years old."

Harrison turned to Santa, surprised. "Jack? He's actually not that bad. He's just kind of dumb and makes stupid choices. And if he's been on your Permanent Naughty List for like a thousand years, then what's the point of ever being good?"

"It's my policy," Santa countered.

"Policy is important," Barack agreed. He certainly knew a thing or two about policies. "But the boy's right."

Harrison locked his eyes on Santa. "The Permanent Naughty List is *way* too harsh a punishment. And I'm not just saying that because I'm on it now. All I'm saying is that even for someone like the Santa Claws Cat Burglar, a lifetime of no presents isn't gonna force him to be good. Sometimes people need an opportunity to do the right thing and be rewarded for it. Because deep down...I think all people are good."

"Well put, son," Barack agreed, reaching out for a fist-bump as Santa stroked his beard, taking in Harrison's words. "Maybe it's time to consider changing the policy. Policies change all the time, especially in this house. And I'm not just talking about our political affairs. I once had a no-dog policy. My girls helped me change my mind on that one." The president made a good point.

"All right," Santa said. "I'll consider it."

"Awesome," Harrison smiled.

Santa stood and nodded respectfully to his host. "Thank you for your assistance, Barry. We should be going." Santa motioned Harrison toward the door. As they headed out, Santa turned back. "President Obama, tell me something. What would you like for Christmas next year?"

"The same thing I ask for every year."

"If I could give it to you, I absolutely would."

"I know, Santa," Barack said with a smile.

"How about an Invisible All-Terrain Super Power Jet Mobile instead?" Santa asked cheekily.

President Obama considered it for just a moment. "Honestly, I'd rather have world peace."

"Says the guy who's never been on an All-Terrain Super Power Jet Mobile," Harrison stated on his way out of the Vermeil Room. He could spend the next thirty minutes making a case for how awesome the Jet Mobile was, but it was time to go home.

54

RETURN TO THE FULWELL HOUSE

Snow fell softly on the White House roof where Santa's sleigh and team of reindeer waited. Reindeer breath hungrily clouded the air as Harrison, Max, and George offered snacks of carrots and apples while Santa chatted with Janice and her Secret Service team.

"I'm sorry for taking advantage of you and asking for all that stuff," Harrison apologized to George. "It was selfish of me."

George playfully tugged on a carrot as Dancer tried to pull it away. "Eh, forget about it. It was fun while it lasted."

"Also, about the Super Power Jet Mobile..." Harrison started. "We left it in Florida. It's in the parking lot of Santa's hotel."

George pulled out her iPhone. "No worries. I'll alert the Elf B.I."

Harrison gently rubbed Dasher's head while the reindeer ate out of his hand. "Why didn't you just say there is no such thing as Naughty Week, especially if you knew you could get in trouble with the BMOC?"

George let Dancer gobble up the carrot. "Okay, look. I never had any brothers. Seeing you and Max and what a good relationship you have and all that…I don't know, maybe I just wanted to be a part of it."

"You know something," Harrison pulled Max into a headlock, "we've never had a sister."

"Yeah, you can come over and play any time you want," Max agreed, struggling as his hair fell over his eyes under Harrison's tight grip.

"Thanks, but I'd have to check with the Big Red Cheese Doodle." George didn't realize Santa Claus was standing right behind her and had been listening to the last part of the conversation, hands on his hips.

"My name is *Santa Claus*, and I wholeheartedly approve. Every good elf deserves a little rest and relaxation with friends," he said as he climbed into the sleigh. "Now let's shove off and get you boys home."

Harrison and Max excitedly jumped into the sleigh, followed by George who made it seem like this was no big deal, but the fact was she had never flown in Santa's sleigh. Not because she was a misfit elf—she simply never had any reason to.

Santa double-checked to make sure everyone was safely aboard, then gave a nod to Janice and the rest of the Secret Service. He tugged on the reigns and—WHOOSH—off they soared into the Washington, D.C. sky.

Harrison and Max screamed with delight at the incredible speed as they banked at the Potomac River and headed north toward Silver Spring.

55

GROWN-UP JOHNNY DOLAN

At the top of Ambler Court, a man leaned halfway in the abandoned lime green SmartCar, burrowed under the steering wheel with the driver's side door open, kneeling on the cold pavement. It was Jack, and he was desperately trying to hotwire the car.

"Come on, come on," he mumbled to himself.

Behind him, eight reindeer brought Santa's sleigh in for a quiet, graceful landing in front of the Fulwell House.

Harrison first spotted Jack. Once the sleigh had come to a complete stop, he climbed out and trotted over to the SmartCar. Santa, George, and Max followed behind.

"Jack?" Harrison said delicately, but Jack ignored him. "I don't think you'll be able to get away this time."

Jack popped his head out from under the steering wheel. "Like you know everything. You're just a kid."

"I may not know everything, but I learned a lot this week," Harrison explained. "Everyone's got a little misfit elf inside him or her. But it's never too late to be good. So you're on the Perma-

196

nent Naughty List, so what? It doesn't mean you are *required* to be bad."

Jack continued fiddling with the wires under the steering wheel, even though he pretty much had no idea what he was doing. The only time he'd ever seen someone hotwire a car was in the movies or on television. But he was committed to the task regardless.

"The Permanent Naughty List is for life, kid," Jack stated, not realizing Santa was within earshot. "And as much as I'd love to get presents every Christmas, it's just not gonna happen for me. It's the hand I've been dealt. The stinky, stinky hand."

Santa took that in. He thought about what Barack said, and he thought about what it might take to change his policy regarding the Permanent Naughty List.

Suddenly the SmartCar started up, surprising everyone. "A-ha!" Jack yawped proudly.

"I bet if you turned yourself in, Santa would consider taking you off the list." Harrison sincerely wanted Jack to do the right thing.

Jack stood and climbed into the car. "Oh yeah, how can you be so sure?"

"Because Santa's right here."

Jack finally turned to find Harrison surrounded by George, Max, and Santa Claus. His eyes gazed upon Santa—feelings of sorrow, resentment, and anger bubbling up.

"Hello, Johnny," Santa greeted kindly.

"Yo, stretch," George said.

Harrison turned to face Santa. "So what do you say?" Harrison asked. He knew he was putting Santa on the spot, but he also knew everyone deserved a second chance in life because, deep down, people were good.

Santa stroked his beard, reconsidering the policy. It wasn't easy for him to make a change without consulting Mrs. Claus, but he knew she would be okay with the decision. She had voiced her opposition to the PNL for years. "Fine," he stated. "I agree to the terms. But it's up to you to make the decision."

Jack pulled the wires under the steering wheel apart, letting the SmartCar's engine die. He got out of the car and broke down. "I was ten! I made ONE mistake! All I wanted was an electric football game, and when Christmas came—*nothing*. My dad told me it was my own fault. He told me to get used to life's disappointments, and by next Christmas, he left me." He buried his face in his hands.

Santa nodded knowingly. These were the kinds of things he dealt with on an annual basis. For many kids, life was challenging. When Jack's father left him and his mom, Jack was pretty much on his own. Jack wiped away tears. "After that, I had no reason to believe in Santa and no reason to be good. So I found another baseball card store and stole whatever I could get my hands on, even Yankees stuff. And I've been nothing but naughty my entire life."

Jack's eyes met Santa contritely. "But I want to change. I want to be good. It's just so easy to be bad. And fun. But I want to turn my life around. I'll do whatever it takes."

"You can start by making the right choice," Harrison stated.

Jack wiped his face and sniffled. "I'm tired of running away from things. I need some positive energy. I've made my mistakes, and I'll pay for 'em. I'm ready to turn myself in." He took a deep breath, a load off his chest.

Santa smiled. "Good boy."

Just then, a mail truck approached, slowing as the mail carrier curiously gazed in their direction. Jack ran in front of it. "You! Hey! Stop!" The truck stopped, and Jack climbed in. "Arrest me. I'll provide you with a full confession of my crimes."

"Hey guy, I'm just the mailman," the mail carrier stated.

"Then take me to the nearest police station," Jack pleaded.

The mail carrier looked at Santa, and Santa nodded at him. "Go on. It'll look good on your Naughty/Nice report, Sam."

The mail carrier looked dumbstruck. For whatever reason, he felt like he could trust the man with the long white beard. "Yeah, sure. No problem," the mail carrier said.

As the mail truck rumbled away, Jack leaned out and waved to Harrison gratefully.

56

GOODBYE TO SANTA

Santa and George walked Harrison and Max back to their house as a cold breeze flowed across the sidewalk.

"Well, I guess this is it," Harrison said somberly.

"Yep. This is it," George said.

Max knew their time with George was running out. He didn't want it to end. "Would you like to come in for some hot cocoa?" he asked. "It's probably not as good as North Pole hot cocoa, but I can give you two bags to make it extra chocolatey."

Santa patted Max on the head. "Very nice of you to offer, Max, but Mrs. Claus is expecting me back in Florida for the New Year, and George is due back at the North Pole. Also, I think your neighbor Mrs. Klopek has already called animal control."

Harrison, Max, and George looked across the street and found a wide-eyed older woman staring out a window at Santa's reindeer.

"Yeah, she's pretty weird like that," Harrison agreed as he reached into his pocket and dug out a folded piece of paper. He handed it to Santa. "Just in case you get lost."

Santa unfolded the paper. "My travel itinerary," he smiled.

"For the record, I did find it," George chimed in. "But not until the boys captured me and held me as their prisoner."

Santa furrowed his brow at Harrison. "I promise," Harrison assured, "from now on, best behaviors. No more shenanigans."

Santa nodded, then turned for his sleigh.

"Santa?" Harrison stopped him. "I was wondering. What do *you* want for Christmas?"

Santa thought about that for a moment. He stroked his beard. Few had ever asked that of him over the years. Finally, he smiled contentedly. "I don't need any presents, son. But the occasional thank you note might be nice."

Santa climbed into the sleigh. George lingered for a moment, enjoying her last few moments with the boys. She wrapped Harrison and Max into a simultaneous hug. "I'm gonna miss you guys."

"We're only a text away," Harrison reminded her.

George smiled at her new friends, then turned for the sleigh. "Be sure to follow me on Twitter. I follow back, no lie! Also, check out this thing called Instagram. I had the idea for this like ten years ago."

"George, you know the policy on social media," Santa reminded her.

"Yeah, I wanted to talk to you about that," George said, climbing in.

They waved to Harrison and Max, and then Santa tugged on the reins. "ON DASHER, ON DANCER, ON PRANCER, AND VIXEN!" and—WHOOSH—the sleigh soared into the sky.

57

MOM'S RETURN

Harrison eyed the clock as he vigorously scrubbed sticky chocolate syrup off the kitchen counter. It was only four thirty, but the sky outside had turned dark. In the living room, Max collected empty chips bags and candy wrappers and shoved them into a trash bag. Between the scrubbing, the running water, and the crinkling of wrappers and chips bags, they didn't hear the door open.

"Harrison? Max? Boys?!" Mom called from the foyer.

Harrison and Max dropped their chores and sprinted toward the sound of their mother's voice, nearly plowing over her with a big fat double hug. Mom squeezed her boys like she was never going to let them go. In the history of hugs, this one might have been the tightest.

Mom kissed and hugged and kissed and hugged and pulled her boys closer. "Oh my gosh, oh my gosh, oh my gosh, I am so sorry, I will never leave you again for as long as I live, I am never, ever letting you go."

"Mom—"

"For the rest of your lives, I will be there no matter what."

"Mom!" Harrison shouted through happy tears. Mom finally released him to look at his face. "We're okay," Harrison assured.

Mom took deep breaths like she had just run a race. "I can see that, yes, but I'm a wreck."

"I'm sorry I ruined your vacation."

"Oh, honey, you didn't ruin anything. At least now we can spend New Year's together," she said as Dale entered with their bags.

"Dale!" Max greeted excitedly.

"Hey, sport!" Dale smiled.

Harrison made eye contact with Dale. "Hi Dale."

"Harrison," Dale nodded, setting the bags down. He gazed at the three of them, still in a tight embrace.

Mom kissed her boys again. "Oh my goodness, what a week." She kissed and kissed and kissed.

"I'm going to head home," Dale said. "Spend time with your boys. I know how much they mean to you. And I apologize for everything—all of this. It's my fault, and it should never have happened. I can't apologize enough." He looked at the boys regretfully. "Boys, I am very, very sorry."

Mom took another deep breath, so happy to be home. "It was a crazy mistake. And once we realized it, you did everything in your power to make sure we got home as soon as possible. I'm just happy the house wasn't burned down." She looked at Harrison square in the eye. "But what happened to the chimney? It looks like a snow mobile smashed into it."

"Snow *machine*," Max corrected.

"Honestly, I don't want to know." She turned to Dale kindly. "I think tonight should just be the boys and me."

"Absolutely," Dale offered. "But first, something for the kids."

Dale unzipped his suitcase and removed a pot and a pan. "Confiscated these from the chalet we rented. For midnight on New Year's."

"Dale!" Mom said, surprised at his thievery.

Dale looked at Mom innocently. "I don't know, I figured it's Naughty Week and all."

Harrison's and Max's jaws dropped to the floor. They couldn't believe Dale, of all people, would celebrate Naughty Week.

"Don't worry, I left some money so the owner could replace them."

Harrison smiled. *What a Dale thing to do*, he thought. But he appreciated the gesture. "Mom? Can Dale come over for New Year's? Maybe hang out long enough to bang pots and pans with us at midnight?"

Mom eyed Dale, surprised at the immense breakthrough. Dale was equally as shocked. Harrison smiled wide, confident that everything was going to be okay.

58

NAUGHTY WEEK: DAY 7

"FIVE, FOUR, THREE, TWO, ONE...HAPPY NEW YEAR!"
Harrison, Max, Mom, and Dale banged pots and pans as
loud as they could. The CLING CLANG CLONG echoed
into the cold, clear night as the stars shined above.

Mom kissed Harrison and Max on their cheeks, then turned
to Dale, smiling. "Thank you for making this week so special. We
will certainly never forget it." She pulled Dale closer and kissed
him on the lips.

"Gross!" Harrison complained.

"Yuck!" Max scoffed.

Mom and Dale laughed, pulling the boys into a group hug.
Over Mom's shoulder, Harrison noticed Mrs. Klopek watching
through her window across the street. "Happy New Year, Mrs.
Klopek!" he shouted.

As Mrs. Klopek disappeared behind a curtain, Mom turned
toward the roof and eyed the chimney. "Okay," she sighed. "I
think I'm ready to know what you guys were up to all week. Start
spilling, boys."

Harrison and Max looked at each other guiltily. Harrison

finally shrugged. "I don't know, we just kinda took it easy—watched TV, played video games, ate a bunch of candy and junk food—you know, that kind of stuff."

Mom smiled warmly at her sons and folded her arms. Clearly this wasn't the whole truth, and moms had a way of knowing.

For moms know...moms *always* know.

59

CHRISTMAS 2013

True to her word, George sent weekly texts to the boys. It was a banner year for the former misfit elf. Santa transferred her to the New Media Division at the end of January and by October she was promoted to supervisor. She absolutely loved her new job. The geeky-cool elves she worked with were like family. She was very happy. On Christmas Eve, Harrison and Max arranged to have special FedEx packages delivered to the New Media Division's holiday party. When George opened the large insulated boxes labeled "Perishable," the scent of cheese and pepperoni filled the air. She nearly fainted when she realized just what had been packed inside the boxes—two dozen piping hot New York–style pizzas.

CITING EXCELLENT BEHAVIOR, Jack was transferred to a minimum-security prison, serving his time for the many burglaries he committed like an absolute gentleman. He set up a little Christmas tree in the corner of his room. Come Christmas morning, a long, flat, wrapped gift was left to him by Santa. He tore it open as soon as he woke up. After so many years, he had finally received the one gift he wanted above all others since being placed on the Permanent Naughty List—a brand new electric football game.

~

THAT CHRISTMAS MORNING, exactly fifty-one weeks after the infamous Naughty Week, Harrison and Max sat in front of the Christmas tree ripping into gifts while Mom and Dale sat close together sipping Christmas tea on the couch. On Mom's finger was a tasteful diamond ring, and Harrison looked up just in time to see her admiring it. He smiled, knowing how happy Dale made her.

Once Harrison started focusing on what was cool about Dale, things changed. The day after Thanksgiving, Dale requested Harrison's and Max's blessing because he wanted to ask their mother to marry him. They responded with a resounding "Yes," and then the only challenge was to keep it a secret until Dale could properly propose on Christmas Eve. Keeping that secret proved to be one of the most difficult things Max had ever done in his young life. On the other hand, Harrison had no problem keeping the secret. He thought it was pretty cool that Dale even asked for their blessing. Dale insisted he didn't want to replace their father. He just honestly wanted to spend the rest of his life with the people who made him the happiest.

Dale lifted his iPhone and started taking video of the boys burying themselves under a sea of wrapping paper. Once Harrison and Max knew they were being filmed, they hammed it up even more. Mom cracked up, and Dale laughed so hard he could barely hold the camera still.

Harrison couldn't remember the last time he laughed so

uncontrollably. It wasn't so much that what was happening was all that hysterical. It was more that Harrison felt genuinely happy. Another Christmas had arrived, and even though he had a tall pile of presents still yet to open, the gift he treasured most, the thing he knew could never be replaced and should never be taken for granted, was his amazing, crazy family.

On the mantle above the stockings stood a framed photo of Dad. He was smiling, and Harrison believed that somewhere out there Dad was watching over things. And smiling.

60

NAUGHTY WEEK: DAY 1

"Calling all unregistered passengers to the Lido Deck," a woman's voice rang over speakers on a sparkling luxury cruise line. Santa and Mrs. Claus—in matching red and white flower print Aloha shirts—climbed the ramp to the main deck with their suitcases. This year, they decided to try something new for their vacation.

"WOOOOO! These two look ready to paaaaar-taaaaay!" a boisterous voice echoed down the galley way. Santa and Mrs. Claus turned to the sound of the voice and found Harrison's and Max's grandmother holding two giant fruity cocktails. She handed them each a drink.

"Well, thank you very much, Geraldine," Santa said smiling.

Grandma squinted at Santa. Did she know him? If she did, she couldn't place it. "Wait, I know you," she said. "Did we meet in Cancun? No, it was last year in Hawaii, right? Or was it Barcelona in '08?"

"Or maybe under the mistletoe sometime long ago," Mrs. Claus suggested.

Grandma looked Santa up and down, then nodded with a sly smile. "That must've been it."

Santa playfully elbowed Mrs. Claus. "We haven't officially met. But I know your grandchildren."

"Harrison and Max? Such good boys," Grandma said fondly.

"Indeed they are," Santa agreed.

"Well, a friend of the fam is a friend of mine," Grandma stated, slapping Santa on the shoulder. "Welcome aboard! Now if you'll excuse me, I've gotta hustle down to the bar and grab a margarita for water aerobics. This is the one week I allow myself to, well, go nuts! Ha! And don't forget—tequila volleyball at noon!"

"We'll be there!" Mrs. Claus hollered.

Santa looked at Mrs. Claus with a bright smile. They clinked glasses. "Happy Naughty Week, Mrs. Claus."

"Happy Naughty Week, Santy Pants."

Thanks for joining Harrison, Max, and George on their naughty adventures! Did you enjoy NAUGHTY WEEK? Here's what you can do next... If you loved the book and have a moment to spare, I would really appreciate a short review. Your help in spreading the word is gratefully received!

A new adventure will be available soon! Get notification of the next book — LUCKY DAY — at mattdonnellywrites.com.

Made in the USA
Columbia, SC
30 November 2020